THE OHANA COTTAGE

MEGAN REINKING

Editing by Librum Artis

Proofreading by Yours Truly Book Services

Cover Design by IndieSage

For Nick, who gave me my own chance at happily ever after.
And for E, A and L for completing it.

CONTENTS

1

MIA

The thing about traveling by yourself is *you literally have to do everything by yourself.* I mutter a curse under my breath as my suitcase, still on the baggage carousel, drags me a few feet forward.

"Do you need help, ma'am?" offers a man who had been in the path of my stumbling feet.

With a sheepish smile, I nod. "Please." I watch as he effortlessly pulls my suitcase off and pops the handle before setting it next to me.

"Thank you so much. I appreciate it," I call to the man, who is already walking away.

I don't like having to rely on other people. I take pride in being a strong, independent woman. I just can't help that I am also a woman who overpacks. Refusing to be discouraged, I heft both suitcases and my carry-on bag onto the cart. After playing a quick game of suitcase Tetris to make sure nothing will fall off, I start pushing the cart to the exit. Walking out of the airport and into the sunshine, I finally take a deep breath. The humid air feels like absolute heaven on my Minnesota winter skin.

As much as I despise traveling, the flight to Honolulu was a great way to start my vacation. I read an entire book and even enjoyed a nice long nap. They also had an impressive selection of classic movies to choose from, so I watched *An Affair to Remember*, one of my all-time favorites. When Nickie and Terry kiss on the stairs of the cruise ship, it's as if time stands still. I get swept up in the emotion every single time I watch it. Despite my current situation, I am still a hopeless romantic at heart.

Vacation might not be the best way to describe this trip, though. After my breakup a few weeks ago, this was more of a last-minute-yet-necessary change of scenery. A chance to invest in some "me time" and figure out what the heck I'm going to do with my life now that Sean is no longer a factor. A mental health reset, of sorts. Yes, that sounds more appropriate.

I needed to get away, and given that it was a whopping 2 degrees back in Minnesota, I wisely chose to come somewhere warm. I'm feeling pretty good about that decision at the moment, given it's 85 degrees here in Hawaii. I make my way to the end of the curb, where the Uber I ordered was waiting for me.

"Ma'am," the Uber driver says in greeting.

Ignoring the fact that I've been called ma'am twice in the last ten minutes, I offer him a smile. "Hi! How are you?"

"Good, good," he replies politely, nodding his head. I hand off the luggage cart and climb into the back seat, peeling off my hoodie and pulling my long, blonde hair to the side so it hangs over one shoulder. Once my seat belt is fastened, I turn my phone off of airplane mode and notice I have three missed calls: two from my mom and one from my best friend, Paige. I send them both a quick text saying I landed and would call them later. Then I turn my phone off and slip it in my bag. I want to soak in my surroundings as we drive. I love exploring new places, and Hawaii has been on my bucket list for years.

Sean and I had wanted to plan a trip to Hawaii for years. Or rather, I wanted. I begged and begged him to go, but we could never make it work with our schedules. I'm wondering now how much effort he really put into it. He always promised it would happen "next year." Now that we've broken up and I needed to get away, Hawaii seemed like the perfect place.

I give the driver the address to my Airbnb and sit back to enjoy the view while we drive. As we ride through town, I take in the towering palm trees and beautiful, bright flowers everywhere. Bushes with the most stunning shades of green line the sidewalks. I inhale a few deep breaths to try to rid myself of any lingering jitters. I'm not crazy like my friends and family said. It's totally normal to fly nine hours by yourself to escape an ex and spend an extended amount of time on a reset, right?

Yup, totally normal.

We pass by a strip of shops and restaurants, and I make a mental note to come back and check out Julie's Coffee and Juice Bar. It's settled in between a travel agency and a cute little bookstore that I'm sure to wander into at some point. I can't wait to come back and explore what this area has to offer. I notice a sign that reads "Farmers Market daily 8 a.m-11 a.m." I will definitely come back for that. All I have for food are a handful of things I bought at the airport, so I plan to come into town as soon as I can.

After about twenty minutes of mentally cataloging all the places I want to come back and visit, the Uber pulls into a neighborhood that has rows of homes on each side. They are all multi-level houses, a mix of white and tan exteriors. Fleeting glimpses between houses tells me we're right next to the ocean. He stops at a house on the right and pulls into the driveway.

"I need to go all the way down the driveway, past the house, please." I had chosen the "Ohana Cottage," a guest house on the same property where the owner of the Airbnb lived. A gravel driveway separates the main house from the cottage, which I will have all to myself.

Climbing out of the car, I slam the door shut and swing my carry-on bag over my shoulder. The driver has already unloaded my suitcases and gives a quick wave as he backs out of the driveway. My feet, still in the sensible sneakers I wore on the plane, crunch on the gravel as I take a couple of steps forward, then pause to take it all in.

The guest house is small and quaint. When I booked, there weren't a ton of pictures of the outside of the cottage, and now I'm wondering if my subconscious had a hand in choosing this place because it looks exactly like something I would dream up. It is a creamy, pinkish color with white beams and trim accenting the windows. There is a white staircase to the right of the house that leads up to the main door. Lush greenery surrounds the entire house, and one big tree to the left of the house extends above and across most of the roof.

I sigh. It is absolute perfection.

After successfully hauling all of my luggage up the staircase (all by myself, thank you very much), I punch the code in the lockbox and pull out the key. Pushing the front door open, a sense of comfort immediately comes over me, almost like I belong here. Slipping my shoes off, I leave my bags in the entryway and move to explore my new temporary home.

I walk straight into the living room, where a couch, loveseat, and coffee table are arranged in front of a small flat-screen TV. There is a set of surfboard pictures hanging on the wall above the TV. I move past the couch and turn right down a hallway, eyeing two doors. The first one is a small bathroom with a single sink and not much countertop space, but it has a shower and a bathtub, which is a win in my book. The last door leads to the bedroom, which is pretty standard—a queen-sized bed is settled under the window in the middle of the room, flanked by nightstands on either side of the bed. There's an upholstered chair in the corner, and a dresser across from the bed, with more surfboard art hung on the wall above it.

I venture back down the hallway to the dining table and kitchen on the right. A booklet on the counter catches my eye. "Airbnb Contract" reads the front page. Inside is a sheet that has all the necessary information I might need. The Wi-Fi password is listed at the top, right above the contact information, and the name John Byrd is shown to be the property owner.

I skim over the house rules, all of which I already read when I booked the cottage. No pets, no parties, no smoking inside, clean house upon departure, etc. The last page is a copy of our contract, with my departure date listed at the bottom. I officially have thirty days to accomplish whatever it is this trip is supposed to accomplish. Thirty days of investing in my mental health. Thirty days of gaining clarity on my relationship with Sean, and thirty days of convincing myself why I am better off without him —mostly so I can convince everyone back at home.

I figure there's no better time than now to get unpacked and settled. I grab my suitcases and wheel them back to the bedroom. Unzipping the first suitcase, I pull out some clothes to change into and transfer the piles into the drawers of the dresser, along with my three swimsuits. I hang the few dresses I have in the closet and stuff the empty suitcases under the bed, then slip into shorts and a tank top.

That done, I grab my sandals and sling my laptop bag on my shoulder and carry it out to the kitchen, where I am pleased to find that the extension cord Paige said was "excessive" was absolutely necessary. Sitting down, I open the laptop and then immediately close it.

Nope.

Work will be waiting for me tomorrow. Today, I am going to the beach to catch my first sunset in Hawaii. I have been dreaming of watching the sun set on the beach ever since I booked this trip. Growing up, I always requested that the first evening of every family vacation would be spent finding a place to watch the sunset. There's just something so fascinating to me that no matter where you are in the world, you're gazing at the same moon and sun. I find comfort in the fact that we're all connected in that way.

Grabbing the keys off of the counter, I slip them into my pocket and skip down the stairs. I already know there's a path that leads to the beach nearby, so I make my way past the main house and quickly spot a sign that says, "Beach Access" between two houses on the left.

Walking down the path, I can't help the smile that's spreading across my face as I take in the beach and ocean in front of me. Sand stretches for about 150 feet before reaching the gorgeous teal water of the ocean, and I can spot a few sailboats in the distance. I am pleased to see it isn't too busy, probably because we are a few miles away from the main public beach access that most tourists use. I find a spot a few feet away from shore and sit down in the sand. The sound of the waves crashing onto the shore is louder than I expected, but ultimately has a serene, calming effect. Inhaling a deep breath, I can practically taste the salt from the ocean on my tongue. Running my fingers through the white sand, I let my mind drift to Sean.

When we broke up a few weeks ago, I felt both sad and relieved, which was familiar territory, since we've been there many times before. This is the third time we've broken up, and we have always ended up drifting back together after a few weeks apart. Sean and I have known each other almost our entire lives. Our moms were best friends, so we grew up with each other, doing playdates and going on adventures together with our families. Even though we attended different high schools, we always stayed in touch, eventually forming the same group of friends. When we were both college students at UMN, we decided to give dating a try—to both our mothers' elation. We fell into an easy relationship, and it surprised us how quickly we went from friends to something far deeper.

It's been four years since we started dating, and I think we both know deep down that this is it. At least I do, anyway. While neither of our families would ever cross that boundary and put expectations on us, Sean and I always felt this pull to try and make it work. I think we were both scared of what life would look like without each other.

The thing about us, though, is that it's just not quite right. There's something missing. It's not that we don't have things in common, or even lack of chemistry, because we definitely have that. We have fun, and it's easy when we're together, but he's not what I see when I think about my future, and I'm twenty-three now—I don't want to waste any more time with someone who I know isn't at least a possibility of forever.

And the biggest reason I chose somewhere far away for this trip is because it's too hard to move on when we see each other all the time, and are in the same circle of friends, all of whom inadvertently remind us of the many memories we have together. I'm determined to let this time away be the best thing for both of us. Maybe we need to live on our own to figure out how to truly say goodbye.

2

MIA

The next morning, I wince as my feet hit the cold wood floors, and I make a mental note to find some fuzzy slippers when I venture into town. The air conditioning in this guest house is impressive. I stretch my arms above my head, let out a yawn, and shuffle down the hallway toward the kitchen. I flip my laptop open on the kitchen table and sit down. Logging into my work email, I find 56 emails needing my attention. I'm an editor for a local newspaper back home, which I absolutely love. I love everything about the writing process, and I love being able to take a decent piece or writing and hone it into something really impressive. And luckily, I can do my job from just about anywhere. My boss is very supportive, and I've reassured her that my work won't suffer while I'm here. I'm responsible for editing the writers' pieces and signing off on them before the newspaper is published that week. Having lost most of yesterday as a travel day, I knew I would have extra work to do today to catch back up.

I respond to the first fifteen emails before heading to the kitchen. I need coffee ASAP, and I pray there will be some in here somewhere. I search the cupboards and come across a coffee machine, along with a jar of ground coffee. The sticky note that's stuck to the top of the jar grabs my attention, indicating when it was opened.

Score! Still fresh.

I set the machine right next to the sink, plug it in, and turn it on. While I wait for the coffee, something catches my eye out the window above the sink. Just off the main house is a pool, and there's a man walking the perimeter with a leaf skimmer. A very muscular, tan, shirtless man. And my guest house kitchen just so happens to have a window that looks directly into the backyard.

Huh. Is that John, the owner of the main house? I wonder if this is a daily occurrence. Is this something I can expect to find out my window every morning? If so, I don't think I will be too upset about it. He lifts an arm to brush sweat away from his forehead, his biceps swelling with the movement. Nope, wouldn't mind at all.

Now, I'm in no place to get wrapped up in another man, but I'm also not blind, so I lean my elbows on the edge of the sink to tilt forward and get a better view. He looks like he's deep in thought as he pushes and pulls the skimmer back and forth on the surface of the water. He looks to be about my age, maybe a little older. His shoulder muscles flex as his arms move, and my eyes trail down to find an impressive set of abs on his stomach.

My phone rings suddenly and breaks me out of creeper mode. Shaking my head to clear my thoughts, I rush over to the table and snatch up my phone. It's Paige.

"Hey!"

"Hey yourself, my Hawaiian princess. Have you had enough of a break yet? Ready to come home?" she asks.

"Paige, I just got here yesterday," I say with a laugh. Paige has been my best friend for years. I actually stole her from Sean. Paige and Sean went to the same school, and I met her at a bonfire at Sean's house in eighth grade. We hit it off right away and have been inseparable ever since. We're both outgoing and friendly. She's a little more on the sarcastic side, while I'm more practical, and we balance each other out nicely. At home, we see each other every day and tell each other everything, so my "break" will be an inadvertent break from her, as well.

She sighs. "I know, just wishful thinking, I guess. I miss you already."

"I miss you too… but I think I'm going to really like it here." I debate telling her about the eye candy that's living just a few yards away from me, ultimately deciding against it for now. Besides, there isn't much to tell. "It's beautiful and so peaceful. You should have seen the sunset on the beach last night. It was absolutely beautiful."

"That's all lovely, and I am totally jealous… but how are you doing, really? You know, with the breakup and everything?"

"I'm fine. Really, I am. I just had enough of all the questions and everyone grilling me about it. I needed to clear my head and get some distance for a while, you know?"

"Hey, you don't have to explain it to me. I get it," she replies. Paige is just about the only person in our circle who is outwardly supportive of Sean and me going our separate ways. Not that she has anything against him—I think she just knows that I'm not my happiest self with him. She knows me well enough to know when I'm not completely happy.

"A break will be good for you. I just don't understand why you had to go all the way to Hawaii. And not bring your best friend… do you know what the temp was today? Negative four! That was the high, for Pete's sake! I'm beginning to wonder why I live here in the first place."

"Ugh, I agree. I'm definitely going to soak up the warmth

while I'm here." I sneak a peek out the window and notice that the man is gone. Darn.

"All right, Paige, I have to get back to work. The time change here gives me a small work window. I'll call you soon."

"Okay, talk to you soon! Send some sunshine our way. "

After hanging up, I pour some coffee into a mug, wishing I had my beloved vanilla creamer to go in it. But black coffee is still better than no coffee. I spend the rest of the day at the kitchen table, buried in my laptop, not able to break away to go pick up some food or even to look outside for another peek at my hot Airbnb host.

The next morning, after applying some powerful sunblock, I pull on a pair of black workout shorts and a matching sports bra. Lacing up my running shoes, I mentally map out a route to run on the beach. I pull my hair back into a high pony and make my way out the door, down the stairs, and past the main house. I make it to the beach access, and the moment my eyes find the sunrise, I have to remind myself to breathe. The sky is blaze orange with streaks of red and pink mixed in. I don't think I've ever seen a sunrise so strikingly beautiful. After allowing myself a moment of admiration for the sky, and taking a picture to send to Paige, I set out on my run.

I run down the stretch of beach, past several resorts, restaurants, and tiki bars. After two and a half miles, I turn around and head back so my run will end up coming to about five miles, just like I run back at home. Out of breath and sufficiently sweaty after the run, I slow down to a walk at the beach access entrance to cool down. Coming up to the main house, I am surprised when I see the shirtless pool guy rounding the side corner of the house with a garbage bag in his hand.

"Hey!" I call out to him, still breathing hard.

He jerks his head up, startled. His eyes narrow at me, and his forehead hardens.

"I'm Mia. I'm renting the cottage in the back. You must be John?"

He continues to stare at me for a few beats, an unreadable expression on his face, then finally nods. He seemed almost uncomfortable or irritated, which doesn't make sense.

Is something wrong? Do I smell? Does he not like conversing with his tenants? Is that against the rules?

Okay then.

"Well, I'm gonna head back to the cottage. It was nice to meet you," I say slowly, still waiting for a response.

His eyes follow mine as I start backing away, but he remains silent. I hold his gaze for a few seconds, wondering what's happening behind those dark blue eyes, but the awkwardness finally gets to me and I turn around and make my way to the cottage.

That was weird.

As I shower, I try not to overanalyze the interaction with John. Maybe he was just in a bad mood? I did surprise him, so maybe he just wasn't expecting to talk to anybody while he took the garbage out. Either way, it seems clear he's not going to be a vacation buddy, and that's fine.

I pull on some jean shorts and a white T-shirt after I get out of the shower, leave my hair to air dry, put sunscreen on again, and call it good. I arranged for an Uber to pick me up once I got out of the shower. I want to explore the town a little bit, and I'm in desperate need of groceries. I've got a few minutes before the Uber arrives, and I fire off a few work emails while I wait.

Once I make it to town, I spend the next few hours roaming. It is a warm, sunny day, so I can't be in a bad mood, even if I tried. I pass a few touristy gift shops and a sunglasses kiosk. When I see Up in the Clouds, the bookstore I saw the day I arrived, I slip in and grab a couple new books to read while I'm here. I love romance novels, and there were several rom-coms available from my to-be-read list. Then I wander next door to Julie's Coffee and Juice Bar. The bell makes a dinging sound above my head as I open the door.

"Aloha!" calls the woman behind the counter, a smile on her face. She has short blonde hair and looks to be in her mid-thirties. She's wearing a gray T-shirt with a black barista apron that has the store logo embroidered on the front.

"Hi!" I say as I approach the counter. "You have such a cute place here! I love it. Can I have an Americano with one pump of vanilla, please?"

"Sure thing. I'm Julie, by the way." We chitchat while she makes my drink. I'm a people person. I can get along with just about anybody. My mom has a running joke that I could make friends on a deserted hike. I guess it's partly due to where I grew up—"Minnesota Nice" isn't just a stereotype; it's a way of life for a lot of people back home.

"What brings you to Hawaii?" she asks me.

"I'm on a solo working vacation. Needed a break from real life after a breakup."

"Oh, I know how that goes," she says sympathetically.

"How long have you owned this coffee shop?"

"About three years now. It keeps me busy, but I love it. It's one of my babies." She turns her back to me so she can grab a lid for my drink.

"You're pretty," a small voice behind me says. I turn to see a little girl with long, brown hair coloring at a nearby table, watching me intently with her brown eyes.

I smile at her. "Well, not as pretty as you," I tell her. Her face pulls up into a smile. I love kids. I'm an only child, so I didn't grow up with siblings, but I babysat all the time in high school. I can make friends with kids just as easily as adults.

"I'm Hazel. That's my mom over there, Julie."

"It's nice to meet you, Hazel. I'm Mia. What are you coloring there?"

"It's a picture of a shark. I love sharks. Do you love sharks?"

"Um, well, I definitely think they're pretty cool... I don't think I'd like to see one in person, though."

"Well, duh." She giggles, and it's so darn cute I can't help but smile.

"Here you are, Mia!" Julie calls, and I turn to grab my drink. "Have a great rest of your day, and I hope to see you again soon."

"You definitely will! Thank you. Bye, Hazel!" I wave to Hazel and make my way out the door. This is the perfect place to bring my laptop to work, and I plan to do that soon. I wander across the street to the Farmers Market, slowly taking my time browsing each table. I grab some fruit, homemade bread, and a macadamia nut granola. On my way out, I pick up a bouquet of flowers to put in a vase on the kitchen table. Loaded down with my bags, I call an Uber and head back to the cottage. Once I've unloaded my groceries back home, I sit down to check in with work for an hour or two. I finished out my first full day by bringing one of my new books to the beach and reading a few chapters while watching the sunset. It is so incredibly peaceful, with the waves crashing into the shore, that I make it a goal to do this often while I'm here.

3

JOHN

I awake with a gasp, hand clenching my chest. *Dammit. Here we go again.* I can feel my heart pounding, not only from inside my chest, but also through my fingertips. Sweat is dripping down my back as I sit up and lean over the edge of the bed. Focusing on taking deep breaths, I hold one hand tightly in the other, trying to lessen the shaking.

It was just a dream. It was just a dream.

Night terrors are nothing new. I deal with them often, although less frequently now than when I was first discharged from the Army six months ago. Up until my tour ended, I was part of a platoon that was stationed in Iraq. A lot of my time there was spent in combat zones, dealing with the constant threat of terrorism on top of engaging with enemy forces. Tonight was the first night terror in about a week, which I'm definitely considering progress.

I've learned a trick to help me through the aftermath; it's

called grounding. I latch onto the first image that comes to my mind: the new cottage guest, Mia. I start cataloging every little detail about her. Her long, blonde hair that was pulled back into a ponytail, her fair skin that was flushed from her run, her crystal blue eyes that had literally stopped me in my tracks. She was about a foot shorter than me, and I guessed her to be around the same age. I inhale a shaky breath, noticing it is slightly easier to take a full breath.

Okay, this is working.

Next, I try to remember the clothes she was wearing—which wasn't much to say the least—as well as her pink Apple watch and her white running shoes. After a few moments, I can feel my head clearing, and my body stops trembling. I force myself to take several more deep breaths until my heart rate seems to be settled back into something more normal. Glancing at the clock, I see it's 3:45 a.m. Knowing I won't be able to sleep the rest of the night, I drag myself out of bed. Might as well make some coffee and start the day. These night terrors always leave me feeling exhausted, but I am never able to go back to sleep.

The kitchen in my house is decent sized, with white cabinets surrounding the perimeter of the room and a large island in the middle. My aunt and uncle had deeded the house and guesthouse to me when they moved to California several months ago. In one of our many phone calls, while I was deployed, they told me they were moving, and they wanted me to have a place to call home. It's paid off, so I just have to pay taxes and utilities, which is fine with me. They moved before I got home, then came back when I was discharged to help me get settled. The military offered to pay me for the first few months after I left the Army, which was enough to get me by. I don't need much. Most of that money is gone now, but I make a decent amount by renting out the cottage to tourists.

Going through the motions to get the coffee ready, my eyes wander out the back window to the cottage. Guilt creeps in as I think about how rude I was to her yesterday. I hadn't meant to not answer her when she was talking to me. What I experienced in combat overseas was life-altering, to say the least. When I came home, I had a hard time adjusting back to civilian life; I didn't know how to relate to people or situations that weren't life or death. Over time it's gotten slightly easier, but it's still hard for me to hold normal conversations. When I do try, I usually freeze up like I did yesterday with Mia. *Especially* when the person I'm talking to is a beautiful woman like Mia.

Sighing, I set my empty coffee cup in the sink, and I head to the bathroom to shower and start my day.

Walking out the sliding patio door, I grab the leaf skimmer from the shed where I keep the pool supplies. Starting on the right side of the pool, I start dipping the skimmer in and sliding it across the still water.

"Hey," says a soft voice from behind me. I turn to see Mia coming across the driveway, a laptop bag on her shoulder and an empty tote bag rolled up under her arm. Most of my body tenses up, but I'm pleased to realize that a small part of me feels relieved she isn't so put off from yesterday's encounter to approach me.

I manage a quick, "Hi."

Her eyebrows raise slightly, as if she's surprised I can speak.

"I forgot to say thank you yesterday for letting me do an extended stay in the cottage."

I give her a quick nod. "No problem."

Apparently, she took those three words as an invitation, because she launches into a whole thing about what she's going to do today.

"I'm heading into town to go to that Farmers Market they have over on Main Street. I got some papaya yesterday, and O-

M-G it was the best thing I've ever eaten in my life. So I'm definitely getting some more of that. Then I'm gonna stop at Julie's. Have you been there? Have you met her daughter, Hazel? She's so sweet. I'm gonna get some work done while I'm there for a few hours, and then I'll be back later."

I wasn't expecting her to say that much. I have no idea why she thought I would be interested in all of that information, and I'm not quite sure about what to do... so I do nothing. I'm frozen in place. I stare back at her, trying to decide how to reply so I won't seem like an asshole. Before I can come up with anything decent, her mouth curls up into a small, shy smile, and she starts backing away.

"Well, have a good day!"

Shit.

Snapping out of it, I open my mouth, but she is already getting into the Uber before anything can come out. *Well, so much for not being an asshole.*

The next time I see her is later that evening. Sitting on one of the chairs by the pool, going through some mail, I turn my head when I hear the cottage door slam shut. I watch her come down the stairs, wearing a dark blue sundress. Her long hair is down and curled, framing her face. She has tan strappy heels on and is carrying a black purse. She is absolutely stunning. I find myself unable to look away from her as she climbs down the last step.

Even though I can't seem to push my lips up into a smile, I force a wave in her direction. This is my opportunity to redeem myself, if I can manage not to screw it up too bad.

She gives me a friendly smile. "Hey, John. How are you?" She comes to a stop at the edge of the driveway. "Julie told me about a local bar not far from her shop, The Toasted Crab. Have you heard of it?"

Of course, I have. In fact, one of my good buddies, Matt, is a bartender there. Before I can answer, she cuts me off.

"I've been here a few days now. I figured I would check out the nightlife."

"By yourself?"

"Of course... who else am I going to go with?"

My jaw clenches involuntarily. I don't like that she's going out by herself. Not that I don't think she can handle herself, because I get the feeling she likes to do things on her own, I just worry about what might happen if the wrong person notices her leaving the bar at night by herself. Hawaii is a relatively safe place, and the locals are great people—but you never know about the tourists. I feel protective of her for some reason. Maybe it's the older brother in me. I want to tell her to be careful, to never let her drink out of her sight, and to wait inside the bar until her Uber arrives when she is ready to come home.

Instead, all that comes out is a strangled, "Have fun."

Dammit, John.

"See ya later!" She waves to me and all but skips over to the Uber. Once again, I watch her leave, and I hate myself for not saying what I wanted to say. I also hate myself because I know there is no way I'm not going to The Toasted Crab tonight.

4

MIA

The Toasted Crab is pretty much what you'd expect from a Hawaiian tiki bar, but in a good way. There is a long, rectangular bar along the far wall and a small stage in the corner. High tops and tables fill the rest of the indoor space, and I notice there is a sliding door that leads to an outdoor seating area, with cute umbrella shades perched over the tables that look like cocktail umbrellas. It's pretty crowded; I don't see any tables open inside or out. I spot an empty barstool on the left corner of the bar and make a beeline to grab it before someone else does.

The bartender comes my way after a few moments and hands me a drink menu, wiping down the counter with a rag at the same time. "You need a food menu, too, or just drinking tonight?"

"Food too, please." I'm starving, but I peruse the drink menu first and find mostly your typical tropical drinks. Lots of piña coladas, margaritas, and six different mai tais to choose from. I order a hibiscus mai tai—when in Rome, right?—and order some grilled shrimp. The bartender is super cute: blond hair, blue eyes, and the tan skin and well-defined muscles that most of the locals seem to have. Must be all the surfing. The register is right next to where I'm sitting, so he starts a conversation with me while he enters his last few customer orders.

"So you're a tourist, right? How long are you here for?"

"How do you know I'm not a local?" I ask, disappointed. I thought I was doing a better job of blending in.

"I was born and raised here; I know all the locals. I'm Matt, by the way. Where are you staying?"

"Nice to meet you, Matt. Mia Taylor. I'm renting the Ohana Cottage from John Byrd," I reply, then immediately curse myself for telling a stranger where I'm staying.

If I get murdered in my sleep tonight, that is definitely all on me. I wonder if I should text my parents and let them know I love them now, or later.

"Oh, John's a good buddy of mine! He does a great job keeping that place in tip-top shape, so you have nothing to worry about," he says. "Just a heads-up—you probably won't run into him much; he likes to keep to himself."

I've noticed that.

"Why's that?"

"It's not my place to say much, but he recently retired from the military. I think he's been through a lot. He doesn't like to talk about it and mostly keeps to himself. I keep trying to get him to come out and hang out, but he doesn't take me up on it too often."

Huh.

"I'll be right back with your drink," he says, tapping the bar top with a grin.

Once he backs away, I settle into people watching. I wouldn't say that I go out by myself often, but that doesn't mean I'm bothered by it. I'm comfortable in my own skin, and I enjoy spending time by myself. I usually start a conversation with whoever is around me—remember, Minnesota friendly—but the barstool next to me is empty, so I can't make a new friend yet.

My mind wanders to John. Taking in what Matt told me, his behavior makes a lot more sense now. He gave off a 'don't mess with me' vibe and seemed like he didn't want to be bothered. But apparently, he has deeper issues that he's working through. My heart tugs for him, knowing what a sacrifice it is to serve our country. It's no secret that soldiers who come home often have a hard time dealing with whatever they experienced overseas.

Matt sets my mai tai on a napkin in front of me. The ruby-red cocktail looks almost too pretty to drink, with a pineapple wedge on the rim and a maraschino cherry on top.

"Thank you!"

He winks at me and goes back to serving his other customers. I sip on my mai tai and go back to people watching. There's a couple sitting toward the middle of the bar that look like they're having a heated conversation about something, and another couple next to them are practically on top of each other, making out. There's a live band setting up in the corner, getting ready to start playing. People start shifting their seats to angle them towards the stage. Matt brings my shrimp over, setting the plate in front of me.

"Enjoy!"

A man slides into the seat next to me, stumbling a little and shifting a few times to find his center of gravity on the stool. One too many mai tais, probably. I tug a shrimp off the skewer with my teeth, savoring the fresh and juicy bite. We sit in silence for a few moments; then he seems to become aware that I'm next to him. He shifts on the stool, and I can feel his eyes creepily scan my body from my face down to my toes. They linger a little too long at my crossed legs, where the hem of my dress has ridden up more than a few inches above my knees.

Ugh.

I'm more bummed out than anything. After being holed up in the cottage working and having very little interaction with others, I was looking forward to meeting some new people. Now it's looking like I might have to call it an early night. I'm not about to entertain some drunk guy who has wandering eyes.

"Hey, pretty lady," he slurs as his body subtly sways from side to side. "You from around here?"

Wow. Minimum effort on pickup, too.

I smile politely, but I don't want to pour gasoline on this fire by engaging in a conversation with him, so I keep my mouth shut. I eat the last piece of shrimp then I pull out my phone, occupying myself with checking emails. I lift my gaze to try to make eye contact with Matt so I can pay my tab, but he's all the way on the other end of the bar, chatting with a pretty woman.

"Can I buy you a drink?" He leans toward me, close enough that I almost gag on the cloud of whiskey that covers my face. Irritation washes over me, and I have to force myself to not scrunch my face in disgust.

"No, thank you. I'm heading out soon."

"Aw come on, sugar, one extra drink won't hurt nothing."

I feel his hand on my arm before my brain can register that he's actually touching me. He doesn't seem to be in a hurry to remove his hand, either. I stare at his hand for a moment, shocked at the contact.

Oh, hell no.

I jerk my arm away and open my mouth to tell him to get lost when suddenly I'm staring at the back of a white shirt. Someone has forcefully squeezed in between us, severing any connection the drunk man had to me.

"She said no," a deep voice says firmly.

John?

I recognize his voice before I glance up and see the back of his head. He's glaring down at my new "friend," his body completely shielding me.

"I think it's time for you to go," he tells the drunk man.

"Hey, John…is there a problem?" Matt questions, looking surprised to see John.

"This guy's had enough; it's time for him to go. He put his hand on her after she told him no."

"Ah, shit, man. I didn't mean no harm. Didn't realize she was with somebody." He makes an attempt to get off the stool, but mostly just falls forward into John. John doesn't budge, his body firmly planted next to me.

One point for John's muscles.

"Why don't you call it a night, man," Matt suggests with an amicable smile but firm tone. He waves a security guard over, who grabs the man by the elbow and walks him towards the front door.

"Wow, thank you, I was about to—" I begin.

John slowly turns to face me, and the look on his face cuts me off. His eyebrows narrow, and he scowls at me. He is pissed.

Did I miss something? Is he mad at me?

"You shouldn't have come by yourself. It's not safe for women to be in a crowded bar by themselves, especially beautiful ones, and especially at night when almost everyone in here is drunk," he says in a low voice, almost like pushing words out of his mouth is painful.

Wait, he thinks I'm beautiful? I make a mental note to process that one later and try to focus on the issue at hand.

"Well, I don't know if you've noticed, but I came to Hawaii by myself. So I literally go everywhere on my own," I say, doing my best to channel some of Paige's sarcasm.

His glare doesn't falter.

My face is only inches from his chest as I stare up at him. This is the closest we've ever been to each other, and from this close I can really see how incredibly gorgeous he is, even when he looks like he wants to murder someone—apparently that person is me?

His short brown hair is styled messily, and he has slight stubble on the side of his face and chin, like he hasn't shaved in a couple days. His face softens only slightly, his blue eyes finding and holding mine for a few seconds. Something starts stirring in my stomach, and I try to figure out what it is.

"Did you come here because you knew I was going to be here?"

"No." Something in his expression makes me question that.

Clearing my throat, I slide off the stool. "Well, I appreciate your concern, and thank you for your help, but I really can take care of myself. I'll see you around."

He moves back an inch or so, just enough to let me squeeze by. My chest brushes against his stomach as I step off my stool, and I try to ignore how good he smells. I make my way out of the bar, feeling his eyes on me right up until I climb in the Uber.

5

JOHN

After I finish cleaning the pool and doing some yard work the next morning, I head back inside the house. I had stayed outside a little longer than normal, hoping to run into Mia. I wanted to apologize for last night. I'm not sorry for wanting her to be safe, but I'm afraid that maybe I came on a little strong.

When I first walked into The Toasted Crab last night, I was focused on taming my anxiety and reminding myself that I could handle being there. When I looked up and saw that scumbag put his hand on her, I almost completely lost it. I'm honestly surprised that I was able to stay as calm as I was, although I'm realizing now that I took some of that anger out on her. Once again, I was an asshole. I seem to be making a habit out of it.

Opening my laptop, I pull up my email and skim the few messages I'd received since last week. My aunt had written to remind me to check on Rose, a neighbor that lives down the street. Rose is an elderly woman who lives by herself. She doesn't have a lot of family in the area, so she rarely has any visitors. I rarely see any extra cars parked in her driveway. When they moved, my aunt had asked that I pay Rose a visit every once in a while. She's a sweet old lady who doesn't ask me a lot of questions about myself, so I don't mind.

I continue scanning through the emails, and my chest immediately tightens when I see a new email from Adam Hanson. My throat feels like it's starting to close, and I swallow the lump that's starting to form. I crack my knuckles and clear my throat.

Nope. Not going there today.

I delete it without even opening it. I'm not ready to hear anything he has to say. Anger rises quickly from deep in my stomach without warning, and I take a deep breath, not wanting it to overwhelm me. My nerves buzz on the surface of my skin, sending a wave of goosebumps over every inch of my body. After a moment, the anger dissipates, and I'm left with just the familiar heaviness in my chest that's simply part of me now. I've learned to function with it and just try my best to ignore it.

After a quick shower, I venture outside and down the street to Rose's house. Rose answers after the first knock, as if she knew I was coming. I have a hunch that she camps out in front of her window a lot, looking outside at the neighborhood, keeping tabs on everyone.

"Rose." I nod my head in greeting.

"John, good morning."

"Need any help around the house?"

"Actually, if you wouldn't mind, this landscaping could use a little help."

"Sure."

I've helped Rose enough that I know she keeps her garden shears in a small shed along the side of her house. Grabbing them, as well as a bucket and a few other tools, I make my way back to the front of the house. She has shrubs lining her front porch that need trimming, and I figure I might as well trim the large tree she has in her front yard for shade. I don't mind the work; it keeps me busy and out of my head.

As I get to work on the shrubs, my mind drifts to the house I grew up in. My dad was always meticulous about taking care of the landscaping at our house, constantly mowing the grass or trimming shrubs. We had a garden in the backyard that required a great deal of maintenance too, so any free time he had, outside of being with his family, was spent doing yard work.

My mom was native Hawaiian, and when they met, my dad adopted some of her cultural values. 'Mālama ka 'aina' means to respect and care for the land. Hawaiians have a deep connection with the islands and find great honor in taking care of them. My father took that seriously, and he took great pride in maintaining a beautiful-looking yard and home for us to live in.

Thinking about my childhood, and more specifically my parents, always hurts and only adds to the crushing grief I live with, so I try and push the memories from my mind. After my parents died, I didn't think grief could get any bigger or more consuming than it was then, but I was proven wrong.

I blow out a deep breath, shake my head, and move on to the next shrub. After an hour or two, I gather the tools and put them back in the shed. I wave to Rose after she pokes her head out and yells her thanks, and head back home.

As I walk into the house and flick on the lights, a tiny sense of comfort comes over me. Since being home, I haven't felt comfortable anywhere, but I feel the least out of place here. In this house alone is the only place I can just be—I can go through daily tasks with my buried emotions, and I don't have to put such an effort into being around other people. It takes an insane amount of effort just to be out there in the land of the living. It's too stimulating for me, too triggering, so I spend most of my time here. That's what my life has come to—living as a recluse.

I strip out of my clothes and step into the shower for the

second time today. Letting the warm water wash over my face, I fight to keep my mind blank and not give in to the wandering that it wants to do. Stepping out of the shower, I wrap a towel around my waist and stop in front of the mirror. I don't look in the mirror too often; my reflection just serves as a reminder of the conflict going on in my head. The darkness in my eyes looks too similar to the eyes of my soldier brothers, and I see those constantly—I don't need another reminder.

I quickly shave, rub a towel over my face, and walk into my room, opening my closet. My eyes catch on my uniform that's hanging in the corner. It's been in that exact spot since I came home, collecting dust. I try and ignore it, like I do everything else. I didn't even put it there—my aunt must have. She washed all of my clothes and unpacked my bag while I was in a post-deployment haze, disconnected from reality. I feel grateful for her and my uncle, but also guilty that they had to see me like that. I know they worry about me.

I slide a shirt off the hanger and pull it over my head. Pulling on some shorts, I fasten the button while walking back down the hall to the kitchen. At the island, I pause and drum my fingers over the marble. Should I call Matt? Maybe see if he wants to come over? It's been awhile since I've seen him, and he knows not to talk about the military around me or ask questions, so he's the easiest person to be around.

I decide against it... maybe tomorrow. I grab my laptop and slide open the patio door to head out by the pool. I drag one of the chairs out from beneath the shade so it's fully in the sun. I figure I can pay some bills and order a couple things I've been needing online. I've been mostly ordering my groceries and having them delivered so I don't have to deal with the grocery store. The sun warms my skin in a familiar way, and I feel calmness trying to ease its way into my body. As usual, it doesn't succeed, and before long, the sun is no longer giving me any kind of comfort, so I head back inside.

6

JOHN

I'm drinking a beer while watching TV that evening, when I hear a quiet knock on the front door. I'm surprised to find Mia standing on my front porch, her hand on her hip. She's wearing jeans and a dark green tank top, and I can't help but wonder if she was always this stunning. She is effortlessly beautiful every time I see her.

"So I was wondering if I have your permission to go into town for dinner tonight? Am I allowed to do that?" She looks up at me with her eyebrows raised and lips pressed together.

Is she being sarcastic?

"I just thought I would make sure that was okay with you, given that I'm just a weak little woman who shouldn't be on her own." She gives me a little scowl that tells me she's annoyed. She looks so damn adorable, and I can't help but be amused, since she's failing miserably at looking menacing. I surprise both of us when the corner of my lip curves upward.

"Um, I actually wanted to talk to you about that. I'm sorry for last night," I say in a low voice.

Her expression shifts from annoyed to surprised.

"You are?"

"Yeah, it's not my place to tell you what to do."

"Oh...well, you're right. Thank you for your apology." She gives me a smug smile. I can't pinpoint it, but there is something about her that intrigues me. Something that draws me in. I don't usually interact at all with my renters, but I can't seem to help myself with her. It isn't just that she's stunning—Hawaii isn't exactly short on beautiful, half-naked women. It's something else pulling me to her. It's like my brain is consumed with an overwhelming cloud filled with memories and painful experiences of combat, but here Mia is, unknowingly making a valiant effort to push her way into that cloud.

"Well, sorry to interrupt your exciting evening," she says, peering past me at the TV before slowly backing down the porch steps. "Unless... unless you wanted to come with me?"

I must look surprised because she quickly pushes on.

"I mean, not as my bodyguard, of course. I don't *need* you to come with me. I was just being nice, as it seems you're not doing anything fun. Anyway, never mind, I should stop talking. I'll see you later!" She gives me a wave and turns around.

"Wait!" a voice that sounds like mine says.

There seems to be this thing that keeps happening when I'm around Mia, where my body responds to her before my brain does. That same thing happens now, when the words "I'll come" fly out of my mouth with zero consultation from my head.

"Oh, great!" Her surprised face relaxes into a smile.

"I'll grab my keys." I turn the TV off and grab my wallet off the counter, all the while wondering what I just got myself into.

≈

Pulling out Mia's chair, I scoot it back in once she sits down. We came back to The Toasted Crab. Not only are they known for their tropical drinks, but they also have killer seafood. It has the best food on the island, in my opinion, and tourists seem to love it, too. I used to come here a few nights a week, and it was the place I missed the most when I was overseas. Besides last night, I haven't been here in about a month. I tried to come meet Matt for a drink, but the crowds and noise just got too overwhelming, and I left before he could even bring me a beer. Hopefully, tonight will go better.

Once I'm in my seat, nerves creep up, and my heart starts slowly racing. I'm uncomfortable being out in a restaurant full of people, even though it's something I did regularly before my tour. It's all different now, and I feel out of place, like I don't belong.

Why did I agree to come? She doesn't think this is a date, does she?

Shit, who was I kidding, thinking I would be able to talk to her for a whole meal? Panic rises in my chest. Luckily, the waitress is by our side and reading off the specials before the silence becomes too awkward. Mia orders a glass of chardonnay. I ask for whatever beer's on tap. The waitress disappears into the back, and I don't see Matt behind the bar, so he must have the night off.

"Good news, I don't see any drunk men around tonight, so my honor should remain intact," she jokes with a small smile.

My lips push together in a tight smile, and I clear my throat, reminding myself to not be an asshole tonight. I am capable of having a normal conversation. "Your Airbnb contract said you're from Minnesota?"

"Yup! I love it there… I could do without the harsh winters sometimes, though. I'm happy to be here."

"Why are you here by yourself?" I force myself to ask her

the question I've wondered since her booking request came through.

"To be completely honest, my boyfriend and I broke up a few weeks ago, and I just needed some space. I wanted to get away to clear my head," she says softly. "Luckily, I have an amazing boss and can do my job from just about anywhere. I'm an editor for a weekly newspaper back home."

I zero in on the fact that she doesn't have a boyfriend, at the same time wondering why I care. I'm not looking for a relationship. I can't imagine letting someone into the fucked-up mess that is my brain. There's no way that would go well. Who would want to, anyway?

"Are you close with your family?"

"My parents died when I was in high school in a car crash. My younger sister, Quinn, and I used to be close growing up, but she had a really hard time after our parents passed away. She left for college and hasn't been back since. We talk every so often, but it's not the same. My aunt and uncle became our official guardians, and I still keep in touch with them. The house and cottage were theirs. They moved to California before I got back." I notice that it feels good to open up and tell her that, even though it's just a small piece of who I am. Losing my parents was devastating, and it was a rough couple of years after they died. Then it was a rough couple of years in Iraq. I wonder if I'll ever *not* have a rough couple of years, at this point.

"I'm so sorry about your parents."

I catch her eyes and give her a hint of a smile. It really is the best that I can do. My shoulders feel tight, and I start to shift in my seat, nervous energy rising within me. My thoughts are all jumbled, and it's hard to cut through them to form a complete sentence. At least I'm trying here, right?

Our waitress brings our drinks, and we both order the Ahi Tuna off the menu. As Mia's ordering, I allow myself to study her a moment. Her hair is pulled back in a braid, and I notice how the dark green tank top she's wearing compliments her eyes. Passing off our menus, Mia's eyes shift to mine. I quickly look away and clear my throat.

"So... Matt mentioned you were in the Army?" she asks hesitantly.

My shoulders tense at the question. Most people know not to ask me about my time in the Army; it never goes well.

"Yup."

"For how long?"

After basic training and some time in advanced training, I was deployed overseas to a base in Germany. From there, we were dispatched to Iraq. After twelve months there, I was promoted to private 1st class and extended my tour for another six months. After those six months, I couldn't bring myself to extend again, not after what had happened. I just couldn't do it. I was honorably discharged and came back home six months ago.

"About a year and a half." That's all I can give her. I'm not interested in opening that can of worms. "What are you planning to do while you're here?" I ask, needing to change the subject.

"Well, work, obviously, but I hope to squeeze in some fun as well. I love the beach. Running in the mornings has been one of my favorite things to do so far. I hope to lounge on the beach some more. I love to read and watch the sunset. I'd also like to go snorkeling at some point too. Oh—and Julie says I definitely need to go hiking. She gave me the name of a few trails."

It seems fitting that she's on a first-name basis with Julie. Something tells me she likes to be social and make friends. Pretty much the polar opposite of how I usually am. How is it that I ended up here with her again?

Our food arrives, and we spend a few silent moments eating. "Wow, this is really amazing!" She says. "The only thing that would make this better would be a side of papaya. That stuff is so good."

I chuckle, enjoying the fact that she loves a small piece of Hawaii that much.

"Do you have any recommendations for things to do while I'm here?"

I shrug and tell her about a few typical touristy things to do. When the waitress comes by, I order another beer before she can give us the tab. For some reason, I'm starting to feel more comfortable talking to Mia. That hasn't happened with a single person since I've been back, and I'm not ready for it to end yet.

7

MIA

Taking a sip of my chardonnay, I glance across the table at John. I'm really enjoying myself tonight. It's been nice getting to know him a little bit, and even though he didn't give me a lot of information, he is a little easier to understand. Between whatever happened in the Army and his parents dying in high school, I can empathize that he's been through a lot in his life.

When I had first invited him to dinner, I never in a million years thought he would accept. I didn't think he'd want to come, honestly. However, the night has been great. I always enjoy getting to know new people. Don't get me wrong—he's still super closed off and kinda looks like he'd rather be somewhere else, but there were a few times where he let his guard down, and I felt like I was seeing a glimpse of who John really was. Not to mention he is insanely good looking. He can sit across from me while I eat any day.

When the server brings our tab, I find myself a little

disappointed. I'm not ready for the night to end. But it's been a long day working, and I'm exhausted. I have another long day of work ahead of me tomorrow, too. John pays, despite my insistence that we split the tab. I thank him and tell him I'll pay next time. He shrugs me off and slips his wallet back in his pocket.

On our way back home, we make some more small talk. And when I say we, I mean me. I do most of the talking, which is not unusual. He seems interested in what I have to say, though. He nods and smirks every once in a while, so I know he isn't too annoyed with me. I glance over and study his face, noting that it is significantly softer than it was at the beginning of the evening. He looks good no matter what, but I think I prefer the more relaxed version of John.

Climbing out and coming around to the front of his car once we arrive, I thank him again for dinner. "You didn't have to do that, you know. I wasn't expecting you to pay. But I did have fun tonight, so thank you. Anyway, I'll see you around. Good night." I start heading slowly for the cottage.

"Good night, Mia."

I almost stop in my tracks. The way he said my name sent a wave of warmth through my body that was unexpected. I turn to see him leaning against the hood of his car with his arms crossed, watching me. Our eyes connect, and I smile, giving him one last final wave.

I cut the papaya in half lengthwise and scoop out the seeds. Cutting it into pieces, I pop a bite into my mouth. Mmmmm. I can't think of a better fruit to go with my cereal for breakfast. I'm developing a little love affair with this fruit; I have some every morning. To me, it seems like the perfect mix between a mango and cantaloupe, and feels quintessentially Hawaiian.

After sending off a few work emails, I figure I should probably check in with Mom. I've missed the last couple of times she's tried to call, and it won't be long before she sends out a search party. She answers after the first ring.

"Mia, dear! How are you?" The sound of her voice makes me smile.

"Hi, Mom! I'm great. How are things back at home?"

"You've lived here all your life. You know how things are. I want to know what you've been up to. What have you been doing? Are you sure this trip was really necessary? Have you met any new friends?" One guess where my rambling comes from.

"I've been doing great, Mom. Really. You don't need to worry," I tell her. "Let's see, lots of working and spending time at the beach. I take a book and read on the sand almost every night so I can watch the sunset. Hawaiian sunsets are unreal! I've made it into town a few times, too—there's a cute little coffee shop I love, and I've been to a few fun restaurants."

I think back to my dinner with John a few nights ago. I haven't seen much of him since then, just a casual wave here and there from across the yard. Oh, there's also the pool cleaning that I stealthily watch from my window around 9:30 almost every morning. Not that I set a reminder on my phone or anything...

"That's great, honey!" she says and then hesitates a beat. "Um, I wasn't sure if I should bring this up…"

"What is it?"

"Well, I was talking to Nancy this morning, and she mentioned that Sean has been asking about you a lot. I'm not sure, honey, but I think he might get in touch with you soon…" she says cautiously.

Nooo.

"I'm not sure where his head is at exactly, but it sounds like he might want to try and work things out with you."

I sigh. "Mom… Sean and I are better off as friends. I think

he's just used to getting back together every time we break up. This is just our routine. We stay broken up for a few weeks and then we always end up trying again. He probably just doesn't know how to move on."

"I know, and believe me, I am on your side. I support whatever choices you make. I'm just giving you a heads-up that he might be calling you soon."

Great. The last thing I want to do is talk to Sean right now. That conversation would go nowhere. I need to somehow have a message sent back through the "mom grapevine" that I'm not interested in getting back together.

"I really don't want to talk to Sean. I don't want to get back together. I'm ready to move on with my life. I've even been on a couple dates since I've been here."

"You have? With who? What's his name?" she asks in surprise.

I hesitate for a moment.

"John." *Shit.* I should have made up a fake name to go with my lie.

"How did you meet him? Are you sure you're ready to be dating? You just got out of a four-year relationship. And don't forget, you don't actually live there. You'll be coming home before too long."

"I know, Mom. Don't worry. John is the owner of the Airbnb I'm staying in. He lives in the main house on the property. And it's nothing serious, just out for dinner a couple times." It isn't technically a lie—we did go out for dinner, but it was just once and not really a date.

"Oh. Okay, well, I trust your decisions. Just be careful, Mia. The last thing you need is to come home with a broken heart."

"I know. Listen, I've got some work to do. I'll call you later! Love you, Mom."

"Love you more, Mia. Bye."

Setting my phone down, I feel a little bad about lying to my mom about dating John. At least I know that the message will get back to Sean. But what harm is there in it anyway? It's not like John will ever know. I just pray that my message will deter Sean from calling. I'm content with closing that door. I knew shortly after we broke up that it was the end of the road for us, and being in Hawaii on my own has only helped solidify that.

The next few days pass by with mostly the same routine. I have my morning coffee with a view, go on a run, and then hunker down to work at the kitchen table or head into town with my laptop and set up at the coffee shop, where I can take my breaks chatting with Hazel and Julie. Then I spend the afternoons either at the shops in town or with my book on the beach. I've been fielding daily phone calls from Paige asking for more details on this mystery man I was supposedly dating. I guess my plan succeeded.

This particular day, I work at my laptop until I can't stay inside for another minute. I grab my book from my nightstand, a beach towel from the closet, and make my way to the beach.

Once I settled on my towel with the book in hand, I find it hard to focus, reading the same sentence over and over. Instead, I close my book and watch people as they play on the beach. There's a couple playing Frisbee, and some kids building sandcastles. Down the beach a ways, a group of people are playing sand volleyball, their shouts and laughter drifting my way.

A mom and son are walking close to the water, waiting for the waves to crash over their feet. Once their feet are covered with water, they giggle and run back to a man who must be her husband. The boy runs into his arms, and he lifts him high onto his shoulders, then puts his arm around the woman, and they continue wandering down the beach.

I smile, noticing a pull at my heart. I want that so bad. The husband, the children, the family… I want it all. I know that by giving up Sean, I'm pushing that dream farther away. Sean will probably ask me to marry him if I go back to him. It's been four years, after all, and most of our friends are starting to settle down. But, if not settling means putting that family dream on hold, then so be it. As much as that sucks, I'm not going to fall back into something that I know isn't right.

My mom's message has made its way into our circle of friends, and Paige told me that Sean knows about me dating. Apparently, there was an in-depth discussion between him and a few of our friends about it. As far as I know, he's trying to move on, too.

My soulmate will find me when the timing is right, of that I'm certain. Standing up, I shake out the towel and gather it in my arms to trek back to the cottage. I'm about halfway down the road to the house when my phone pings with a text message in my pocket, and as I fumble to try and pull it out, I accidentally drop the book on the road. I bend down to pick it up, thinking that I should really get one of those cute beach bags in town.

"Mia!"

I freeze.

I know that voice. But why is that voice here? Slowly rising, my eyes look up, and my mouth drops open.

My mother.

Paige.

In Hawaii.

Standing in front of John's house.

8

MIA

"Surprise!" Paige shouts as she runs towards me to give me a hug. Mom waves enthusiastically as Paige's arms pull me out of my trance.

"What in the world are you guys doing here?" I stammer, still shocked, but able to walk to where mom is standing.

Mom gives me a sheepish smile. "We just wanted to come check on you and make sure you're really doing all right! You know there's only so much you can gather from a phone call. Don't worry—we'll only be here for a few days, and you'll hardly notice we're even here."

"Isn't that great?" Paige asks with a gleeful grin.

"Now, come show us where you've been staying!" Mom says while picking up her small suitcase and backpack. Paige loops her arm in mine, and we start walking down the gravel driveway toward the cottage. Still in disbelief, I try to wrap my head around the fact that they're actually here. Mom is a few paces in front of us when I hear her say, "Oh! Hello! You must be John?"

Shit. Shit. Shit.

"Mom!" I run to catch up to where she's standing, and I see John sitting by his pool with his laptop. He shuts his laptop and slowly gets to his feet, a wary expression on his face.

"Oh, you don't have to get up!" I say, panicking at how fast this situation is unraveling. "I know how busy you are. Come on, Mom—the cottage is this way…"

"Mia! Don't be rude!"

I sigh. "Mom, this is John. John, this is my mom and my best friend, Paige."

John manages a smile and a small wave, which I appreciate since I know that's more than he offered me when we first met.

Not wanting to stay and see what kind of questions my mother has for him, I hurry them along. "Come on, this way. I can't wait to have you try some papaya! See ya later, John." I throw a quick smile his way and then herd mom and Paige toward the cottage stairs.

"Damn. Is that who you've been dating?" Paige whispers once we're out of earshot. "I approve!"

"Shhh!" I hush her and open the door, letting them inside my humble abode.

"Where exactly were you guys planning to stay? With me, I'm assuming?" Not that I mind, I'm happy to see them.

"Well, your contract mentioned that there was a pull out couch, so that's perfect for me. And we figured Paige could just stay with you in your room? Is that all right, dear?" Mom asks expectantly.

"Sure, that'll work." It's not like I can ask them to go stay in a hotel. There's no point in wasting their money when I have the space for them here. Not a lot of space, of course, but we can make do. They already flew all the way here; I might as well make the most of it.

"Here, let me show you where my room is. You can keep your stuff in there."

I give them a quick tour and help them get settled; then we reconvene in the kitchen area. "Should I make us some margaritas?" I had picked up some margarita mix while I was in town yesterday, wanting to bring a cocktail with me to the beach one of these days.

"Why not, that sounds lovely," Mom replies, and Paige's face lights up.

After I hand everyone a drink, Mom wastes no time jumping right into her interrogation. "So! That John boy is sure handsome, what's he like? You're sure you're in the right headspace for seeing someone new? Have you heard from Sean at all?"

"Sean who?" Paige mutters, sipping her margarita as she peeks out the window toward the pool and John, turning to wiggle her eyebrows at me.

"Mom, I've been here for almost two weeks now. Sean and I broke up a few weeks before that, so it's been over a month. I'm truly over our relationship, and honestly, that happened pretty soon after the breakup. I knew in my heart that we weren't right for each other."

She looks at me for a moment, then reaches across the table and squeezes my hand. "Okay, if you say so, sweetheart."

"So what should we do tomorrow? Beach?" Paige asks, finally joining us at the table and thankfully bringing a change of subject with her.

"That sounds nice; we can have a picnic lunch! Oh, let's invite John! I'd love to get to know him!" Mom says.

My eyes widen slightly, not sure how to respond. "Oh, Mom. I don't know. He's pretty busy. And he's a local. The beach is nothing new to him."

"Well, you won't know until you ask, dear."

"I can ask, sure."

My mind starts running, wondering how I'm going to successfully manage to avoid John for the next couple of days while they're here. There's no reasonable excuse that I can use to deter them from hanging out with the guy I told them I was dating—especially since he lives right next door. And I can't exactly come clean and tell them I lied in the first place. Especially since everyone back home already knows. It would be mortifying if they found out I made it up.

"Great! Now, I'm exhausted from traveling, so if you'll excuse me, I think I'll go take a shower and get ready for bed. I hope this was a good surprise, Mia," Mom says, rinsing her cup out in the sink.

"It was! I'm glad you guys are here." I give her a quick hug. "I'm gonna run over and see if John wants to join us tomorrow. I'll be right back!" I race out the door and slam it shut behind me before Paige offers to come with.

Ugh.

What am I gonna do? I walk slowly over to the house, trying to think of a way out of this situation. John's not out by the pool anymore, so I walk up to the front door and knock. When he opens the door, he gives me a warm smile, and damn if my heart doesn't skip a beat.

"Can I come in for a minute?"

"Sure," he replies, opening the door wider for me to come in.

"Sorry about earlier, I didn't know they were coming. They surprised me. I know I only booked for one person, I hope it's not a prob–"

He cuts me off with a shrug. "It's fine."

"Ok, great. Thanks. Um. One more thing…" I sigh, embarrassed by my backfiring tactics.

"What is it?" His eyes narrow in confusion.

"So, I was wondering if you wouldn't mind helping me out with something…you know I mentioned that I broke up with my boyfriend before I came to Hawaii?"

He nods.

"Well, apparently, he might want to get back together, and when my mom mentioned that a few days ago, I knew that I didn't want to talk to him, so I kind of told her a little white lie to keep him off my back."

"Okay...."

"I told her that I'd been dating someone here."

He looks at me with a raised brow.

"But I haven't."

"You told your mom you've been dating when you actually haven't?"

"Yes... and here's the kicker... I kind of—accidentally—told her it was you I was dating." I gave him my best nervous smile, trying to appear confident, like this stupidity happens every day.

"Me?" His brows lift in surprise.

"Yes. And now they want to go to the beach tomorrow, and they asked if you would want to come, and I'm not really sure how to get myself out of this mess... so I was wondering if you might be willing to do me a favor and come with us? Maybe go along with the lie that we're dating? If you don't want to, I totally get it. It's a lot to ask, I know. And I'm sure I can just tell them you have other plans, but they're just going to keep asking."

He looks like he's struggling to find the right words. "Uh... I'd really like to help you out, but... I don't know... I'm not good at playing games. I'm sorry."

"Oh, no problem," I say in a rush. "I totally get it. Forget I even asked!" My cheeks flush with embarrassment.

What did I really think he was going to say? It took him multiple contacts before he even spoke to me, and I want him to meet my mother?

"Okay, I'll see you around then. Good night!" I rush out the door before he can say anything else. Running back to the cottage, the shame washes over me in full force.

Ugh, kill me now.

I turn the lock on the door behind me, creep past my sleeping mom on the couch, and shut the lights off on the way to my room. Paige is just getting ready to crawl into bed.

"Okay, spill," she says as she pulls back the covers on the left side of the bed. "I've been keeping it PG in front of your mom, but now I want all the details. Have you kissed him? Have you hooked up? He's seriously hot!"

I turn the light off and climb under the covers on my side of the bed. We've been friends for a long time, we've had quite a few end-of-the-night chats about boys in our day, so this is certainly familiar territory. I just don't know how much to say, and I hate lying to my best friend.

"Yes, Paige, I am aware of how hot he is. He's also a really nice guy. He's kind of closed off, though, and he hasn't opened up much." This is all true.

"Why's that?"

"He's been through a lot in his life. His parents died when he was in high school, and then he just got out of the military a few months ago. I think he's still processing a lot from that."

"That sucks. I totally get it, though. Post-deployment can be really, really hard." Paige would know; her dad is a former Air Force pilot. She was pretty young when he retired from the Air Force, but she's mentioned a time or two how challenging it was for him and their family.

"Yeah, for sure. Let's get some sleep. I'm glad you're here, Paige. I missed you," I whisper, not able to fight my heavy eyelids any longer.

"Missed you, too. Night."

∽

"Are you sure John can't join us?" Paige asks while gathering towels for the beach.

"Yeah, he wishes he could, but he has stuff to take care of

today." I throw my book and sunscreen into the communal beach bag my mom brought.

"Bummer, maybe we'll catch up with him later. We can have dinner or something!" my mom offers, looking excited again.

"Yeah, maybe." *Except probably not, because we're not actually dating, and I'd kind of like to crawl under a rock and never speak to him again after last night.*

"All right, is everybody ready? Paige, you packed a cooler with lunch and drinks, right?"

"Yup! We're good to go."

We climb down the stairs and walk toward the road. Just as we are about to clear the main house, the slam of a front door closing has all three of us looking to the right.

"Hey." It's John, wearing blue swim trunks and a white tee, coming our way with a beach towel under his arm.

"Oh, John! Are you able to join us? We packed extra sandwiches just in case, so we have plenty of food!" Mom offers.

"Yup, thank you." He gives her a tight smile.

Did I miss something?

I give him a questioning look.

He meets my eyes for a second and then falls into step next to me as we resume walking. I slow my pace slightly to let Mom and Paige get a bit ahead of us.

"What are you doing? I thought you didn't want to play games?"

"I just said I'm not good at playing games; I never said I didn't want to help you." He offers nothing more.

"And now you're going to help me anyway?"

"Yup. I still don't think I'm the best person for this. You should have asked Matt; he would have been great." Although he says that with a slightly pained look.

I smile. "Well, thank you. I appreciate it. And just so you know, I don't usually play games either. I'm just desperate for it to look like I've moved on."

"I get it," he says and then glances over at me. "Have you not moved on?"

"I have. I'm totally over my relationship; I just haven't started dating anyone else yet. I made that part up."

He nods.

We venture onto the beach and walk a little way down to find a clear spot to set our things. John knows the owner of a beach chair rental place, so he offers to go grab us some. I offer to go with since that would be something that someone who was interested in dating him would definitely do. Plus, he took his white tee off, and I can't bring myself to part with his biceps.

"Do you make it to the beach very often? I bring a book here almost every afternoon, and I never see you," I ask while we walk the beach.

"Not really...too many people."

I nod. "You're really not a people person, are you? Not that it's a bad thing. Just an observation."

"I guess you could say that."

I don't want to push him, especially since he's already doing me a favor, so I don't ask any more questions. We get to the beach chair stand, and we grab four chairs as well as an umbrella. He somehow manages to carry three chairs and an umbrella while I carry one.

Once we make it back, we arrange the chairs into a line and stick the umbrella in the sand in between Mom and Paige's chairs. I slip my swim cover off and push my chair back so I can lay flat. After Paige and I help each other apply sunscreen, I lay down on my stomach, prop up on my elbows, and position my book under my face to read.

Before long, Paige has fallen asleep, mom is engrossed in her own book, and John is staring quietly at the ocean. Taking in the sound of the waves, I try to focus on my book, but it's hard to concentrate because I'm constantly sneaking peeks at the man next to me.

9

JOHN

"Beer?" Mia reaches into the cooler and hands me a Gold Cliff IPA. "I noticed this was what they gave you at The Toasted Crab, so I picked some up when I was in town grabbing my margaritas the other day. Figured I'd give it a try." She reaches back into the cooler and grabs one for herself.

"Thanks." I like that she remembered what I ordered. "It's my favorite."

Mia's mom closes her book and shifts to turn her attention to me. "So, John, did you grow up here?"

"Yes, ma'am."

"Oh please, call me Mary. Does your family live close by?"

"Mom—" Mia started with a warning tone.

"It's okay… No, they don't. I don't have any family close by. I don't mind, though. I like being on my own." I push myself up out of the chair. "If you'll excuse me, I think I'll go for a swim." I don't want to be rude by shutting down the conversation, and I hope I didn't come across that way. I have to go along with this charade because I can't seem to say no to Mia, but that doesn't mean I'm okay with a lot of personal questions.

"Oh, sure, dear."

I make my way towards the water. The first familiar wave hits my feet, and I feel almost like the ocean is giving me a hug. I grew up in this ocean, but haven't been swimming since I've been back. I venture deeper and dive under the water. Surfacing, I tread water for a few minutes, wondering why I didn't force myself to do this sooner. After every minute that passes, I feel like I can take a slightly deeper breath. I hadn't even realized that I was holding that much tension.

Nothing about myself feels the same as it did before I went overseas. It's like once you join the military, you're not only committing to serving your country, you're also committing to trading your soul and going home with a completely new one, with no instruction manual on how to live with it. Even if you don't experience anything particularly traumatic, it's almost impossible to not be changed by your time in the military. I can feel the first sting of tears in my eyes, and I shake my head, trying to make it stop. When this happens, I do my best to shove it down as far as possible. If I let those emotions come to the surface, I won't be able to stop. It's easier to just push it down and bury it. I glance back toward the beach and spot Mia. She isn't hard to miss—she is an absolute knockout in her black bikini. She had pulled her hair up in a bun, and her skin is developing a nice tan in the time she's been here.

I wonder why I am so drawn to her that I couldn't say no when she asked me to help her out. In general, saying no to people is a lot easier than saying yes, so it shouldn't have been a problem for me. But once again, I shocked myself by going along with it. It's not like it's a huge hardship to pretend to be into her, though—that won't take much effort.

I swim back to shore and walk out of the water, shaking the

water from my hair. I glance up to see both Mia and Paige with their mouths slightly open, staring, then Mia is shushing her friend, as if she said something inappropriate. Now, I'm not conceited, but I am used to women giving me attention. I know enough to know I've always been attractive, and I've gotten good at ignoring the stares and comments. Mia liking what she sees is different, though.

We spend the next couple of hours lounging, eating the sandwiches they brought for lunch, and swimming in the ocean. I manage to avoid any deep questions, and I hope I just came across as quiet and not rude. I hate to admit it, but this day has been really great for me. I actually enjoyed myself a little bit. We start packing up when the girls are ready to head back. I had let my buddy know where our chairs would be, so we didn't have to worry about returning those. After gathering all our stuff, we start trudging towards the access point. I let all the women go in front of me, and when Mia passes me, I have a sudden urge to put my hand on her back.

Wait, why not? Isn't that what I'm supposed to be doing? Showing that I'm into her?

That's reason enough for me. My hand finds her low back, and I lightly press as she walks in front of me. Damn, it feels good to touch her. Her eyes fly to mine in surprise, and I give her a reassuring smile. After a few moments, I reluctantly pull my hand away.

"Have fun today?" I ask, falling into step next to her.

"I did! Did you?"

"I did, actually. Thanks for inviting me," I say with a wink.

She gives me a sweet smile, and I'm immediately captivated by it. I wonder what else I can do to make sure I see that smile again. Once we make it back to the house, Mia's mom invites me over to the cottage for dinner. A part of me is exhausted and ready to hole up in the house by myself for the night, but I'm not quite ready to say bye to Mia yet.

"Sure. I can run into town and pick up some food if you want?" I offer.

"Oh, that would be great!" Mary replies.

"Are you sure?" Mia looks up at me with a guilty smile once her mom and Paige were out of ear-shot.

"Yeah, no problem."

"Okay, great. I would offer to go with you, but I really need a shower."

"That's all right; you have my number, right? From the contract sheet? Text me what you guys want, and I'll go grab it."

"Sounds good!" she replies, walking toward the cottage. "Thanks!"

I veer left to head in the house. After a quick shower, I pull on some khaki shorts and a white button-down. Grabbing my keys off the kitchen counter, I drive into town to pick up the food. Once I make it back, I walk to the cottage and knock on the door. I feel slightly awkward knocking on the door, given I own the place, but I want to be respectful of their space. Paige answers with a smile and lets me in, taking the bags of food from me.

"Oh, good! I'm starving! Thanks again for picking it up," she says while placing the food on the kitchen table.

I nod.

Mary is in the kitchen, blending up some margaritas. "Hi, John!"

"Can I help with something?" I ask, walking into the kitchen.

"No, Mia's just finishing up in the shower, and then we can eat."

Still feeling like I should do something, I walk further into the kitchen and open the cabinet to pull out some plates.

"Paige, did you borrow my brush?"

I turn with the plates in my hands, and my eyes immediately find Mia in the hallway, wearing nothing but a towel. My mouth goes dry, and I grip the plates tighter.

Holy shit.

Her skin is still damp, and her hair is a tangled mess. She glances in the kitchen, and her eyes go wide in horror when they land on me. Her cheeks flush red, and she clutches the towel tighter, starting to retreat backward down the hallway.

Paige smirks in amusement, her head turning from me to Mia. "I did; it's on your dresser in the room."

Mia turns and runs the rest of the way, slamming the door behind her. I clear my throat and blink a few times, then remind my legs to move. I bring the plates to the table. Mia eventually emerges from her room wearing shorts and a tank top, hair still wet but brushed through, not a trace of makeup on. She slides into the chair next to me. It takes her a few minutes to get over her embarrassment, which I find amusing, but it doesn't take long before she's back to her normal chatty self.

"So how's Dad? What's going on at home?" she asks her mom.

"Your father's doing great. It's been really cold this winter, so work has kept him pretty busy." Mary glances at me. "Mia's father owns an HVAC company, and they're always busy this time of year doing maintenance and repairs on furnaces. Minnesotans need their heat to work, after all."

I smile and nod.

"So what kind of things have you two been up to? Mia said you went out to eat a few times, is that right?"

Mia jumps in before I can answer. "Yup, we've been to a couple restaurants. John took me to his favorite place, called The Toasted Crab. They have the best Ahi Tuna I've ever had in my life." As she's speaking, she reaches her arm out and rests it on my forearm. Her touch sends a shock wave up my arm, and I try not to tense or react in an obvious way. My heart beats a little faster.

Did she feel that too?

I peer over at her to see if I can gauge any sort of reaction, but her face gives nothing away. Eventually, she removes her hand, and I can't help but notice my arm feels colder. We finish dinner, and I help clear the table.

"Well, ladies, thank you for letting me hang with you guys today. It was fun. I'm gonna head out."

Mary and Paige both wave goodbye, and Mia offers to walk me to the door. As we approach the door, I can feel two sets of eyes on us, watching our every move. I smile down at Mia and put my arm around her shoulder.

Too much?

She stiffens for a second, but recovers quickly and slips her arm around my waist. I place a quick kiss on her forehead. The contact sends a shiver down my spine. When I pull back, there is no questioning this time whether she felt that too. Her blue eyes are wide with surprise and a hint of something else—longing maybe? Her eyes lock with mine for a few seconds, until I reluctantly release her. I give one last smile and step outside. Shutting the door behind me, I walk to the main house, thinking about how good it felt to hug her.

It's obvious there is something between Mia and I, but what does it mean? Is it just attraction? Chemistry? Either way, I don't think I'm in a good headspace for any of it. I wish there was some way to keep taking the relief she gives me from my pain while still keeping her at arm's length. I don't want to drag her down with me. It's not fair to her, and I refuse to do it.

I blow a breath out and shove my hands in my pockets as I walk past the pool and in the patio door. As much as I enjoyed myself today, it was also the most human interaction I've had in one day since I've been home. I'm exhausted, and a bit overwhelmed. I shuffle to my room and fall on the bed, falling asleep within seconds of hitting the pillow.

10

MIA

Apparently, John rendered my body useless, because I stand staring at the closed door for longer than a few seconds, completely frozen in place.

What just happened?

My mom clears her throat behind me, and I spin around, seeing both her and Paige watching me expectantly. Paige is fanning herself obnoxiously, and I manage to roll my eyes.

"Well, I think it's time to call it a night," Mom announces. "Tomorrow's our last full day; we go home the day after that, so let's get some good rest so we can enjoy tomorrow!"

I nod, coming back down to earth. "Yes, good idea."

We retreat to our bedtime routines for the night. When I come into the room after brushing my teeth, Paige is sitting up in the bed, waiting for me. "What's the matter, Mia? You look a little frazzled?" she teases.

"I'm just tired. The sun really took it out of me today."

"Uh-huh, sure."

Not wanting to field any more questions, I shut the lights off and crawl into bed. It doesn't take us long to fall asleep.

The next day we make plans to head into town so I can show them around the cute little shops I've been frequenting. I wanted to let John off the hook, so I told them he had other plans for the day. We arrange for an Uber to come pick us up, and we leave without any sign of John in the main house. While in town, our first stop is obviously Julie's. We grab some coffee drinks and a couple muffins. I introduce them to Hazel, who fills them in on the latest book she's reading about jellyfish. Mom and Julie hit it off right away, chatting until our drinks are ready.

I take them to Up in the Clouds, although they don't really appreciate books like I do, and I'm the only one who leaves with a book. We have lunch at a little tiki bar along the beach and then hit up a couple gift shops, where they pick out a few souvenirs to take back home.

On the ride back to the cottage, I feel proud of myself for managing to avoid any major questions about John. However, my satisfaction is short-lived, because John is doing yard work outside when the car pulls into the driveway, and Mom all but springs out of the car.

"John! Nice to see you. Would you like to join us for dinner tonight? It would be wonderful of you to show us that crab place you love so much." John visibly tenses, and I see the struggle in his eyes as he contemplates what to say. My stomach clenches, and I try to come up with something to let him off the hook. I open my mouth, but John beats me to it.

"Sure."

Sure?

Ugh, I feel terrible for roping him into doing something he

doesn't want to do—again. "Are you sure? If you're busy, we totally understand…" I make eye contact with him and try to convey that he doesn't have to if he doesn't want to. He just holds my stare and takes a deep breath.

"I'm sure. Let me take a shower and get cleaned up." He starts gathering his tools, while Mom and Paige start walking towards the cottage.

"Great!" Mom says. "See you in a bit!"

I stay where I am because it's suddenly necessary to get a read on what he's thinking and make sure he's okay with this. When Mom and Paige begin climbing the stairs of the cottage, I step closer to John.

"You don't have to do this, you know. I can just tell them you forgot you had other plans."

He looks at me. "It's fine. They're leaving tomorrow, right? This is the last chance to pretend we're dating?" I nod. "Then let's do it. I'll meet you out here after I shower." I'm still hesitant but agree and walk back to the cottage to get changed.

Forty-five minutes later, we meet John outside where he had backed his car out of the garage. My mom and Paige fill the car with chatter on the way into town, filling John in on the events of our day. When we arrive, John holds the door open for us as we pass by him into the bar. I find myself hoping he'll touch my back again this time, and when he does, it makes my stomach flip. I give him a quick smile, and he visibly softens, almost as if my smile had an effect on him. That softness is short lived, though, because The Toasted Crab is absolutely packed, and I instantly worry this might be too much for John. Matt sees us from behind the bar and waves.

"Should we go outside and see if there any tables available out there?" I suggest. I think John likes that suggestion, because he leads the way outside. My mom and Paige follow behind him, and I take up the rear. The doors to outside are right next to the bar, and as we pass by, I hear Matt call for me.

"Hey, Mia!" I turn towards him and step up to the bar, letting the rest of them go on without me.

"Hey, Matt. How's it going?"

"Great, we're slammed tonight, though. How the hell did you get John to come here on a Saturday? It's the busiest night of the week. I don't even ask him to do anything on the weekend anymore 'cause it's an automatic hell no. You must have superpowers, girl." My stomach sinks because last time we were here, it was a Tuesday and not nearly as crowded.

"Shoot, I hope it's not too much for him," I say with a wince. "I better go check on them. We'll come say hi later, okay?"

"You better." Matt smiles and gives his attention back to his customers. I turn just as the others are coming back inside.

"No luck," Paige says, scanning the room for an open table. "Oh! Quick! Those people are leaving; hurry and grab that table!" She scoots around me and manages to grab one of the chairs, smiling proudly. I glance at John, and his face is drained of all color, and he looks like he's about to be sick. I shoot him an apologetic glance and move to sit down. I resolve to make this dinner go as fast as it possibly can so he can get out of here. Mom sits next to Paige, and John sinks into the chair next to me. I put my hand on his thigh and squeeze lightly, trying to be reassuring. He looks down at my hand and then up to my eyes. His stress seems momentarily replaced with something else, and I'm suddenly aware that my hand is still on his leg, and maybe that's exactly what I should be doing in front of my mom and Paige, but I also really don't know if he's okay with that. So I take my hand away and bring it to rest on my lap.

The hostess appears with menus. "Hey, guys! I'm so sorry, but we're slammed and short staffed tonight, so anything you want to order, please do so at the bar, okay? We'll bring any food you order out to you here." We each take our menus and peruse them for a few minutes. Once everyone knows what they want, I offer to go place our order before John feels like he has to.

"I'll come with," Paige says, standing up. We walk up to the bar, and squeeze in between a couple stools. We eventually get Matt's attention and he saunters over, eyeing Paige the entire time it takes to get to us.

"Mia, who's your friend?" he asks while one corner of his mouth is turning up into a half smile.

"Matt, this is Paige. Paige, this is Matt." Paige smiles politely and then starts rattling off our order, either completely oblivious to Matt's stares or ignoring them all together. She tucks a strand of her shoulder-length brown hair behind her ear, and I watch in amusement as Matt follows her hand the entire time. I'm not surprised. My best friend is stunning. She has an olive skin tone that I would die for, and her hair is a rich chocolate brown shade that compliments her pretty green eyes. Guys hitting on her is nothing new, but it still makes me smile.

"You got it. Need anything else?"

"Nope, that should do it."

"We'll bring it over when it's out." He winks at her and turns around to enter our order. We start walking back to the table.

"I'm surprised he wasn't full on drooling. Did you see the way he was looking at you?" I tease Paige. She rolls her eyes.

"Ugh. Shut up. Bartenders flirt with everybody; it's part of their job." We make it back to the table, and I slide back into my seat. The first thing I notice is John's leg bouncing as he taps his foot against the floor. He's rubbing his hands together under the table, and his face is tight with anxiety.

"Excuse me," he says, pushing his chair back as he stands up. I watch him as he heads to the hallway that houses the restrooms. I give him a few minutes and then excuse myself. This whole situation is my fault, and I need to make sure he's okay. The restrooms are all the way at the end of the hallway, and I stop about halfway down to lean against the wall and wait for him. When he finally comes out, he locks eyes with mine, and he slowly comes to a stop across from me, leaning against the opposite wall. I watch him inhale a deep breath. I take a step closer so I'm in the middle of the hallway.

"I'm so sorry, John... I didn't realize it was gonna be this busy, or I never would have let you come. I feel so terrible, I should have never put you in this positi—"

"Mia," he cuts me off and then continues in a rough voice, "I just need a minute... it's a lot. The noise, the people, everything." At that moment, some girls come out of the women's bathroom, and I need to scoot closer to John to let them pass. We're now about a foot away from each other, and it's hard to ignore the current that hums between us. It's so thick I can almost hear it. I'm sure he doesn't feel the same thing happening —he's probably preoccupied with whatever's going on. And I'm being superficial by focusing on something as petty as being attracted to him, when I should be giving him space to work through whatever he's feeling. Feeling guilty, I start backing away to leave.

"I get it...I'll leave you alone so you can—" My words stop when he grabs my wrist. I glance down at his hand and then look up to find his eyes locked on mine.

"Can you stay?" he pleads, his eyes so full of torment that I can't help but hold my breath. I realize in this moment that I just might agree to anything he asks if it might take some of the pain away.

I nod. "Of course," I whisper. I move so I'm right next to John, our arms touching, and I lean myself against the wall too. I'm not sure exactly what he needs in this moment. Should I talk to distract him? Or should I stay silent and give him some peace and quiet? I opt for silence, hoping that my presence alone is what he was asking of me. After about five minutes, I can see his chest rise and fall out of the corner of my eye as he takes a couple deep breaths. He pushes away from the wall and turns to face me with a timid smile on his face. His face and eyes look slightly more relaxed then just a few minutes ago. My eyes lock with his, and I search for anything he'll give me.

"Let's go," he says. I nod and follow him out of the hallway and back to our table. As soon as we sit down, our food arrives, and we dig in. I inhale my food, trying to speed this up as fast as I can. I can see John take a few deep breaths, but overall he's a trooper. He even joins in the conversation a little bit. When we're done eating, John gets up and goes to the bar to pay before I have a chance to offer to do it myself. While he's there, I rush my mom and Paige to finish their drinks.

"You don't want to stay for one more?" Paige asks. I shake my head. "No, I'm exhausted. Let's go back to the cottage." They reluctantly agree, and we stand up just in time for John to join us to walk out of the bar. As we walk to John's car and further away from other people, I finally release the breath I didn't realize I'd been holding.

Once again, Mom and Paige do most of the talking on the drive back. When we arrive, I thank John for dinner and give him a hug goodnight. I hug him for a beat longer than I normally would, to hopefully convey how sorry I am for how the night went... or maybe it was for purely selfish reasons, I'm not exactly sure. He gives me a reassuring smile as I back away toward the cottage, waving goodnight.

11

MIA

The next morning, I make my guests some scrambled eggs and cut up some fruit. I savor our last breakfast, knowing that they'll be leaving in an hour or so... but I also can't help when my mind wanders to John and when I might be able to see him again. I hope he's not too mad at me after last night. After we eat, I clean up the kitchen while they finish packing up their suitcases. When I put the last dish in the dishwasher, I arrange for an Uber to come pick them up from the cottage. "Are you sure you don't want me to come with you to the airport?" I ask again.

"No, there's no sense in that. We can manage fine!" Mom says, zipping her suitcase. I help them carry their bags down the stairs and toward the main road. While we're waiting for the car to arrive, Mom turns to me. "Mia, I just want to say that I was wrong. I thought it was too soon for you to get involved with someone else, yes... but it's obvious that you two have something special. I don't think I've ever seen you look at Sean the way you and John look at each other. It's obvious you two have chemistry."

I blush and push my lips together in a tight smile.

"Just be careful. I guess I'm still not sure how this is going to work long term. You will be coming home, right?"

"Of course. Don't worry so much, Mom. I'll figure it out," I say, knowing that there is, in fact, nothing to figure out. John isn't interested in me; he was just playing a part. I will just need to remind my heart to stop reacting to every little thing he does.

"I love you both, and thank you for coming to visit me," I say with a smile.

Behind me, I hear the door of the main house open, and John comes down his front steps. He smiles at me then turns to my mom and Paige.

"I just noticed you were out here with your luggage. Just wanted to say bye. It was nice to meet you both."

"Oh, John. It was a pleasure," Mom says while wrapping him in a hug. I can see him visibly tense. "Take care of our Mia while she's here, okay?"

John nods and takes the opportunity to slip his arm around my waist.

Easy, heart.

"Will do," he replies. His hand is burning through my clothes, and I try not to fixate on the sensation.

The Uber comes into sight down the road, and once it comes to a stop we all move to help load the suitcases in the trunk. I give my mom a hug, tell her I love her again, then turn to give Paige a hug.

"I demand all the juicy updates," she whispers in my ear. Then she smiles at John and hops in the car. John and I watch as the Uber backs out of the driveway and disappears down the street. I blow out a deep breath, nearly crumbling with relief. It really was nice to see them, but I am glad to have some time to myself again that doesn't involve an entire subplot of faked romance.

Speaking of... "Thank you for going along with the whole dating thing. I still feel awful about last night. I know it was stupid, but I really appreciate it."

The corner of his mouth pulls up into a smile. "It wasn't all bad. What are you up to today?"

"I have a little bit of work to do that I put off when they were here. Then I'm not sure. How about you?"

He shrugs. "No plans."

"Well...I'm sure I'll see you around." I give him a small smile and start toward the cottage.

"See ya."

I make it a few steps, then glance back to see John firmly planted right where I left him, watching me walk away.

A few hours later, I pull on an oven mitt and grab the sheet of cookies from the oven. After working for a few hours after Mom and Paige left, I ran into town and grabbed some cookie mix so I could bring some to John as a thank you. I set the pan on the top of the stove and leave the cookies to cool for a few minutes on the baking sheet. Then I head to the bathroom to double-check my appearance.

Not that I'm trying to impress him or anything... but maybe I am? I stop in front of the mirror in the bathroom and assess myself. I'm wearing a cream-colored tank top tucked into a sage green skirt that looks killer with my blonde hair, if I do say so myself. Okay, it might be a little fancy for a cookie delivery, but I'm all right with that. I even throw on a little lip gloss for good measure.

Back in the kitchen, I set the cookies on a plate, throw some foil over the top, and make my way out the door. When John answers his door, he looks almost happy to see me. But then again, maybe my heart is just making that up.

"I made you some cookies to say thank you again." I hold up the tray and smile.

"You didn't have to do that." He steps to the side to let me in. I walk in and set the plate on the kitchen counter. He comes to my side and peels the foil off the plate. "I love cookies. Want one?"

"Sure! I did steal one already, but I'll totally have another one. They're pretty good!"

He grabs a cookie and backs up until he's leaning against the kitchen counter, facing me. I lean against the kitchen island, directly in front of him. We take bites of our cookies and steal occasional glances at each other.

"Sorry about last night," he says. "I usually try to avoid crowded places if I can help it."

I shake my head. "John, you don't have to apologize. I totally get it. And it was my fault. I should have just had an honest conversation with my mom instead of dragging you into this."

He shrugs it off and changes the subject. "So, was it nice having your mom and Paige here?"

"It was. I definitely miss them... but it's also kind of nice to have my quiet cottage back." I glance up, and my gaze connects with his dark brown eyes. He slowly nods, and I can't seem to break my eyes away from his, like there's something holding them in place.

"Do you want to stay for dinner? I was just gonna grill a steak, but I can make an extra one if you want?"

"Sure," I reply, our eyes still locked together.

He finally breaks the trance we're in and heads for the fridge.

"I have stuff for salad over at the cottage; I can run and grab it real quick? I would love to offer to bring some papaya, but I'm all out. I need to run into town tomorrow to grab some."

He chuckles. "Salad sounds great. I'll turn the grill on and prep the steaks."

"Perfect, I'll be right back with the salad."

I run back to grab the salad, and on the way back, I spot John in the backyard setting the steaks on the grill that's on the patio next to the pool.

"I'll bring this in the kitchen and put it together for us," I tell John. He nods.

In the kitchen, I peek in the cabinets, searching for a salad bowl and a cutting board. I find what I'm looking for just as John comes back into the house. I start cutting the lettuce, and he grabs a bowl on the counter that has some gorgeous tomatoes. Coming beside me with another cutting board, he starts slicing them for the salad, throwing them in the bowl with the lettuce.

We work in silence, but I'm surprised to find that it's a comfortable kind of silence. I usually like to fill any lulls in conversations with small talk, but I get the sense that John prefers the quiet. I don't mind it so much, either. John goes outside to flip the steaks while I grab some plates and utensils to set out. I like his kitchen; it's much more spacious than the one in the cottage. The kitchen table is cluttered with mail, so I neatly pile it all together and set it on one corner of the counter, hoping he doesn't mind.

"Ready to eat?" he asks, bringing the steaks inside.

"Yes! That smells delicious!"

He hands me a Gold Cliff from the fridge, and we make our plates and sit down. I go to the far side of the table, and John sits right across from me.

"Oh, wow. This is good," I say, taking my first bite of steak.

"Glad you like it."

We eat in silence for a few minutes, then I glance around until my eyes land on the pool outside. "Do you swim in the pool a lot?"

"Not a lot. Just every once in a while. Do you like to swim?"

"I do. I always wanted a pool growing up, but my parents would never agree to it. There are only a couple months out of the year when it's nice enough to swim outside, so it really isn't worth it. Apparently, they're a lot of work to maintain too. You need to clean it, what, every day?" I try to act like I am guessing instead of confirming the fact that I watch him every morning like a total creeper.

He nods. "You're welcome to use this one any time you want, you know. While you're here, consider it yours, too."

"Really?" I ask with excitement. That certainly wasn't part of the lease agreement. "Do you offer that to all of your tenants or just me?"

He looks up from his plate, and thinks for a moment, then looks back down. "Just you."

Oh.

"Well, thank you. I will definitely take you up on that."

We eat the rest of the meal in our comfortable silence, then I clear our plates and bring them to the sink. I start rinsing them to put in the dishwasher as John brings the salad bowl over. He places his hand on my back between my shoulder blades as he sets the bowl next to the sink. I freeze and instinctively hold my breath.

Is he really touching me? Why? No one's here to pretend for.

He removes his hand and backs away to clear more dishes, while I seem to be stuck in time.

What does that mean? Was he just being nice? I'm sure I'm overreacting. Just go with the flow, Mia. Stop rambling to yourself.

We finish cleaning up dinner without any more touching instances. I look around at the clean kitchen. I'm not quite ready to call it a night yet, so I turn to John.

"I'm not ready for bed yet. Do you want to sit out by the pool? Ooh, better yet—how about I go grab my suit and take you up on that swimming you offered? You already gave me free rein, no backsies!"

He snickers. "Knock yourself out."

"Will you join me?" My boldness surprises me. Maybe the beer has made me gutsy? I'm well aware that I'm tip-toeing around a line that maybe he doesn't want to cross. But I'm also a firm believer that if you want something, you should go for it instead of just waiting for it to fall in your lap. Did I want John? I'm not gonna get all caught up in overthinking anything. All I know is I like him, and I like being around him. I look across the kitchen at him expectantly.

After what seems like forever, he nods. "Sure."

12

JOHN

I grab two more beers from the fridge and head out to the pool. I changed into my swim trunks while Mia ran to get her suit on. To say I'm starting to have second thoughts is an understatement. It's becoming harder and harder to resist this pull I feel towards her, and I'm not sure if being in the pool half-naked is a good idea. But hell if I was gonna turn her down when she looked so excited to swim.

I sit on the edge of the pool, dangling my feet in the water as I set our beers on the concrete next to me. I think of all the times I used to swim in this pool, and how it just doesn't feel the same now. Nothing does. It's like there's this gray undercurrent that makes everything else seem less vibrant and not as interesting. It's the strangest thing. I remember how I used to feel, and I'm aware that the way I'm feeling isn't normal, but I just can't shake this fog enough to allow myself to feel that way again.

The cottage door slams shut, and I smile at Mia as she comes across the driveway toward the pool. She has pulled her hair up into a messy bun and is wearing a black coverup dress and flip-flops. She looks so genuinely happy, and I've never been more jealous of a person's emotions in my life. I wish I could find a way to be that carefree again.

She walks over to me and pulls the coverup off to reveal an olive green one-piece suit. I force myself to not stare and focus back down at the water, but I can't think about anything other than the fact that she's so close. Next thing I know, she is a green blur flying past me as she jumps into the pool, the water splashing my legs. She surfaces, takes a big breath, and smooths her hair from her face.

"This is amazing. The water is so warm! What a beautiful night, huh? I wish we could see the sunset from here." She treads water and looks up at the sky. It's just starting to get dark, and she looks mesmerizing with the water reflecting around her. She swims over to where I'm sitting and pulls herself up slightly onto the ledge, resting on her elbows, and reaches for the beer I brought her. I watch her take a sip, unable to take my eyes away from her.

"Do you ever get lonely living here all by yourself?" she asks, looking up at me.

Actually, I try my best not to feel much of anything most of the time. I realized pretty early on after coming home that if I leaned too much into any emotion—happy or sad—that it was a slippery slope. It was too easy to spiral into the memories and drown in the anger, sadness, and grief. I've been living in this dull gray area where I don't feel much of anything. I've been comfortable there.

"No."

She looks up at me, as if waiting for me to say more. When I don't, she gives me a small smile and swims backwards. As if there is some magnetic force between us, I can't stop my body from pushing off the edge and slipping in the water. I don't want her to shut down, but I also don't want to talk about me.

"So why did you and your ex break up?" I ask.

She swims to where she can touch, but the water is still up to her neck. She leans back against the pool wall and shrugs.

"We weren't right for each other. We've broken up several times over the years, one of us always initiating it. There was never any big reason. We didn't fight over anything... I think we both just had periods of time where we wondered if we would be better with someone else. I broke it off this time. In the past, we always ended up back together after a few weeks apart. Not this time, though. I'm ready to move on for good."

I nod.

"When was your last relationship?" she asks me.

"I was dating a girl about a year before I was deployed. Nothing too serious. Nothing since."

"Why not?"

No one's been able to pull me out of my fog the way you seem to.

I shrug.

"What's your type?"

You.

I shrug again, not quite sure how to respond. I'm okay with small talk, but when it comes to expressing myself, I usually shut down. It just happens automatically. Our eyes meet from opposite sides of the pool, and I hold her stare, wishing I could silently tell her everything I want to say without having to say it out loud. She gives me a small smile and starts swimming slowly towards me.

"I think I have you figured out." Her eyes narrow, like she's thinking hard.

"Oh yeah?"

"Yup." She stops a few feet in front of me, running her hands over the top of the water. My heart starts beating faster.

"Care to enlighten me?" My eyes stay glued to hers.

"Well... you're a good guy, for one. I've seen you over at Rose's, helping her out. You like to keep to yourself most of the time, and I never see any friends over here. You don't open up to many people, and if I ask you a question too personal, you shut down. You like the ocean, but you don't go to the beach very often—too many people. Gold Cliff is your favorite drink, and The Toasted Crab is your favorite place to eat."

She comes a few inches closer, my heart beating even faster, like it does every time she's this close. She looks down, as if she's suddenly shy.

"And... I think that maybe you like me, but you won't admit it." She glances up and locks eyes with mine again.

My mind goes blank while I think of how to respond. She misinterprets my silence and starts backing away, but my body refuses to let her put more distance between us. My hand seems to agree, because it reaches out to grab hers. She stops and lets me come closer until my face is only inches away from hers, my hand still clutching hers. I twist my hand and thread my fingers in between hers. I typically haven't liked to be touched at all, but this feels good. Instead of my body tensing, it almost seems to relax a little.

"I think you might be right," I force out, looking down at the water. I can feel her eyes on me.

"About which part?"

"All of it," I say quietly, bringing my eyes back up to meet hers.

She closes the space between us until our bodies touch, our stomachs brushing against each other in the water, and one of her knees between mine. My breath hitches, and all of a sudden, my brain is working overtime.

This isn't a good idea. You're not ready for this, John. It won't be fair to her.

She interrupts my rambling brain by leaning in and pressing

her lips to mine. My heart jumps, and my body instinctively takes over. My hand reaches up to cradle the back of her head, and the other hand comes to rest on the swimsuit fabric on her hip. She brings both of her hands to the sides of my face as our lips move against each other.

Damn, this feels good.

She presses herself tighter against me, squeezing the back of my neck. We continue to kiss until my brain starts up again.

Don't do this, man. You're not good enough for her.

I reluctantly break contact and press my head to her forehead, both of us breathing heavily.

"Mia... you don't want me." It comes out rougher than I intended.

She raises her eyes to mine, foreheads still connected.

"What if I do?" she whispers.

"Mia..." I force myself to put some space between us, even though every single cell in my body is screaming to do the opposite.

"I'm... working through some stuff. You deserve somebody who can give you more than I can. Trust me... I'm not good enough for you."

I swim to the pool stairs and sit on the second step from the top, running my hands over my face, feeling like an asshole again for crossing that line. She spends a moment staring at me and then moves my way. She swims slowly then sits down next to me, our arms brushing against each other.

"I think you shouldn't be so hard on yourself, John," she says quietly. "I'm not asking for anything serious, and I'm not expecting anything."

I shake my head. "I'm not good at opening up, as you've noticed. It's hard for me. I'm not good with people."

"That's okay. I'm good with people, so I'll be great for both of us," she says with a small smile.

I manage a half-smile.

"Whatever this is..." She waves her hand in between us. "Let's not label it. No pressure. Let's just see what happens."

I nod, contemplating what she's saying. "I think I can handle that." I'm not sure if I can, but she makes me want to try. I shift so my body is tilted toward hers. I feel the urge to open up to her, even if I can only give her something small. "There's something about you, Mia. I feel more comfortable with you than anyone else. You make things easier for me, for some reason."

Her face lights up. She smiles, then rests her head on my shoulder.

"I'm glad," she says.

She grabs my hand and slips her fingers in between mine, letting our arms hang down so they touch the water, while she brings her other arm across her body to hook onto my arm, squeezing as close to my side as she can. I let myself soak it in, because her touch feels so warm, so comforting. We spend the next half hour sitting on the step, snuggled together, dangling our feet in the pool. We stay mostly quiet, as if she understands that I'm the most comfortable that way. Eventually, she stands and grabs her towel and coverup. She walks back to me and plants a kiss on my cheek.

"Goodnight, John." She starts walking back to the cottage.

I watch her as she walks away.

"Goodnight, Mia."

13

MIA

The alarm on my phone is annoyingly persistent, and after a few moments, my eyes reluctantly open, and I blink a few times, staring up at the ceiling. I stretch my arms above my head, and when the memory of last night pops into my head, I smile. That was hands down the best kiss of my life. I wonder how much time I'll have to wait before I get to kiss him again, because I can easily see that becoming addicting. I had been slightly embarrassed to make the first move, but I knew without a doubt that John would never kiss me first. Even though he seemed hesitant about it, I am ultimately happy with how the night ended. We're just going to see where things go. I'll be heading home in a couple weeks anyway, so I'm not looking for anything serious.

Forcing myself to get out of bed, I brush my teeth and shower, run a brush through my hair and pull on a gray cotton romper. I walk into the kitchen to make some coffee when I notice a note lying on the rug by the front door. It looks like it had been slipped underneath the door. Picking up the note, I read the words "Enjoy."

Confused, I open the door. On the mat is a plastic bag I recognize from the Farmers Market. Peeking inside on my way back to the kitchen, I find three papaya. I let out a little laugh. I grab my phone off the counter and find John's number.

Mia: Thank you for the papaya :)

It only takes a few seconds before I see the three dots indicating he is typing.

John: You're welcome. I knew you were out.

Mia: You saved me from making a trip into town. I appreciate it. What are you up to today?

John: Thinking of taking my surfboard to the beach. Want to come?

Mia: Yes! Can I have an hour to get some work done first?

John: Sure. Come over when you're ready.

I fly through as many work emails as I can in the next hour, responding to writers who have questions about specific articles they're working on. I even squeeze in a quick twenty-minute conference call with my boss, and when she hangs up, I shut my laptop.

After lathering up with sunscreen, I quickly change into my black swimsuit and pull the romper back over top. I slide my sunglasses on top of my head and reach for my book, then change my mind. There is no way I'll be able to concentrate on a book if John is around, let alone shirtless on a surfboard.

I venture over to the main house and knock on the sliding door by the pool. John appears from the hallway and waves me in. He's wearing no shirt and black board shorts that go incredibly well with his broody face.

"Hi," I say with a smile.

"Hi." He stares at me from across the room, the intensity in his eyes creating butterflies in my stomach. "You ready?"

"Yup!"

He leads me past the kitchen to a door that opens into the garage, where he slips on his sandals and grabs his surfboard. We head toward the beach, walking slowly, soaking in another beautiful day in paradise. As we pass by her house, I wave to Rose, who's sitting on her porch.

"Hi, Rose!" I call. I haven't talked to her much. She's not outside often, but she always says hello to me if she's out on her porch.

"Hi, dear!" She waves and smiles. I turn my attention back to John.

"When's the last time you've been surfing?"

"Right before I left for basic training, I guess."

"You haven't gone since you've been back?"

He shakes his head.

"Why not? Too many people?"

"Just haven't felt like it."

Okay then. I guess that's all I'm getting.

We walk the rest of the way in silence. Once we reach the water, I find a spot to sit and watch as John carries his surfboard into the water. I keep my eyes glued to him for the next hour or so while he paddles out, finds the perfect wave to surf all the way near shore, then turns around and does it again. He's mesmerizing. He does it so effortlessly, with such ease, that you can tell he's been surfing for a long time. I wonder why he hasn't been surfing since coming home. Surely there are times when the beach is less crowded, right?

Eventually, he walks out of the water, and the sight of him carrying his surfboard, drops of water running down his well-defined abs, sends a shiver down my spine. He's out of breath when he sets his board down and drops down next to me.

"Have fun?" I ask him with a smile.

"Yeah, that was fun," he replies, still taking deep breaths.

I study his face while he stares out at the ocean. He looks significantly more relaxed, his face is much softer than before. I wonder if he knows he has a scowl on his face most of the time. Thinking that maybe he'll be more apt to talk if he's more relaxed, I decide to try my luck.

"Has it been hard to do certain things since being back? Even things you used to do all the time?" I ask cautiously.

He sighs, then nods. "Yeah." He looks at me, opening his mouth like he wants to say more but isn't sure what to say. I wait patiently, and eventually, he gives me more.

"It's hard to explain. It's not the actual activity that's hard— it's just... the thought of being out in the world around other people makes me not want to go in the first place. It's overwhelming if there are too many people or too much going on." His eyes drop to the sand in front of him, and a sadness washes over his face. "Also, it doesn't seem fair... doesn't seem *right* for me to just go back to normal life when..." He stops, rubs his face, and goes quiet for a moment. "When so many couldn't."

My heart tugs in my chest, breaking for him and everything he must be dealing with. He turns to me and offers me a small smile.

"You make it easier, though."

Well, there goes any chance I had of not completely falling for him. My heart is now firmly on Team John.

I smile back at him. "I do?"

He nods. "Yeah." I let that sink in for a minute. I like that I make things easier for him, even though I have no idea what I'm doing that's so helpful. There must be more that I can do.

"What else have you been wanting to do but haven't yet?"

He sighs, turning his gaze back towards the water.

"Well, I used to fish a lot. My buddy Brian is a guide, and he owns a deep-sea fishing charter company. We used to go out when he had time between his client charters. He's invited me along a couple times since I've been home, but I always end up turning him down."

"I'll go with you if you want."

His brows lift high in surprise as he looks over at me.

"You would do that? Do you like fishing?"

"Well, not really. But I've never been deep sea fishing before, and I'm up for trying anything once."

I would do just about anything if there was a chance it would help lift some of his burdens. Fishing isn't exactly my idea of a great time, but if he is willing to dip his toes back into living a full life—and I apparently help him do that—then that's exactly what I want to do.

He looks at me in disbelief.

"Really?"

"Of course."

He smiles the biggest smile I've ever witnessed on him—granted, it still isn't a whole-face kind of grin, but it's darn close. He puts his arm around me, pulling me in while he plants a kiss on my temple.

Yup, I'd definitely do anything to see that smile.

"Well, if that's all it takes to get a kiss, then let's go fishing every day!" I say, feeling flirtatious.

He chuckles.

I'm serious.

I hold his gaze, and his eyes soften. He lifts my chin, brings his mouth to mine, and then rests his hand on the side of my head, his fingers getting tangled in my hair. My whole body tingles in response to his kiss, and I wrap my hand around his smooth, firm arm.

Yup, I could get used to this.

He pulls away from me with a smile and finds my hand to thread his fingers with mine. I rest my head against his shoulder, and we sit in silence, watching the waves crash onto the shore.

When we get back to the house and cottage, I take John up on his invitation to work by the pool. I grab my laptop and get situated on one of his lounge chairs next to the sparkling blue water. I spend the rest of the afternoon doing my work in the sun, taking a few breaks to cool off in the water. John goes to check on Rose and comes back an hour later after helping mow her lawn.

When it starts to get dark, he makes us some sandwiches for dinner and walks me back to the cottage, giving me a quick kiss at the door. He's almost to the top step when I feel my chest tighten, not wanting to see him go. "Hey…" I call out. He turns halfway around, eyebrows lifting as his eyes meet mine. "Do you want to come in? Maybe watch a movie with me?" I hope my voice doesn't sound as desperate as I feel. I just want to be close to him.

He smiles and comes back in my direction. "I would love to."

"Great!" I reply, making my way inside. "How about I make some popcorn while you pull up movies on the TV?" I haven't even turned the TV on since I've been here, so he would know how to work it better than I would.

"Sure."

I pop a bag of popcorn in the microwave and pour it into a bowl.

"What kind of movie do you want to watch?" He asks from

the couch. I grab us a couple Gold Cliff's and join him, placing the bowl on the coffee table.

"What kind of movies do you like?" I ask him. "I mean, I'm obsessed with classic movies, especially romance ones. I watched *An Affair to Remember* on the plane; have you ever seen that? Oh my gosh, so, so good. But don't worry, I won't force you to watch one of those." I pause to take a breath. "We can watch something that you like?"

He smiles at me, and I realize I was rambling a bit. I feel my cheeks heat up and smile sheepishly. He grabs my hand, threading his fingers through mine, and rests them on his leg.

"I'll watch whatever you want to watch," he says. "I'm not a big movie guy, so seriously, whatever you want. I'm just happy to be here."

My cheeks heat up again, this time flushing along with a smile I can't stop from forming. "Are you sure? You may regret that decision in a little bit." He laughs and hands me the remote. I'm surprised at the huge selection of movies available to choose from. He gave me permission, so I choose the romance section. Up pops a long list of all my favorite movies.

I gasp. "Ah! *The Notebook*. Tell me you've seen that, right? You probably got roped into seeing that in high school." I'm talking mostly to myself, which I'm aware of and okay with. "And *Gone With the Wind*! A classic for sure, but way too long for tonight. *The Princess Bride*! Yes, let's do that one!" I haven't seen it in a while, and it seems like a good choice. Maybe John will appreciate the sword fights. John gives a nod of approval, and we settle into the couch, eating the popcorn on my lap with our free hands.

After about an hour, I glance over to see John fast asleep, his head tipped slightly to one side. I press pause on the movie, untangle my hand from his, and gently shake his shoulder.

"John," I whisper. His eyes flutter open, and he jerks a bit before his eyes clear and he looks at the TV.

"I turned it off. Figured we should call it a night."

He nods and stands, tugging me to my feet. At the door, he gives me a hug and kiss on the cheek. When he's gone, I put the popcorn away and get myself ready for bed. I fall asleep with a smile on my face... the same one I've had all day.

14

JOHN

"How are things going there?" Quinn asks when she calls the next morning.

"Good," is my reply. I wish I could say that it was easier for me to open up to family, but it's not. It might even be the opposite. Quinn would be the very last person I would want to unleash all my shit onto. She's been through enough in her life; the last thing she needs is to take on my issues too. After high school, she attended the University of Alaska Anchorage. I think being in Hawaii was too hard—too many memories of our parents—so when she had the opportunity, she fled and hasn't been back since.

I don't blame her; I left via the military. How somebody goes from one extreme to another, like Hawaii to Alaska, is crazy to me, but that's Quinn. She's strong-willed and independent; when she makes up her mind, there's nothing stopping her.

She's a sophomore there now, and absolutely loves Alaska.

She checks in at least every week. I think she can tell that I'm going through some shit, but there's not much she can do from so far away. I don't like that she worries about me; it makes me feel guilty. I appreciate when she calls so I know she's all right, but I don't want to talk about myself to her, either. I usually find an excuse to cut things short, like I do now.

"Quinn, I gotta go. Let me know if you need anything, okay?" I hear a sigh, and then "All right... bye, John." I hang up and hop in the shower.

As I'm just finishing dressing, I hear a light knocking on the patio door. I was expecting Mia, but I'm surprised to see a little girl with her as well.

"Hi, good morning!" Mia says cheerfully. "So guess what? I was at the coffee shop this morning, and Julie got a call from her sister saying she broke her arm and needed help getting to the hospital. So Julie starts shutting the whole coffee shop down, kicking everyone out, and tells Hazel that they need to go. Well, I felt bad that Hazel would be stuck at a hospital all day, so I offered to watch her for a few hours! John, this is Hazel. Hazel, meet my friend John."

Mia moves to her side, and the little girl peers up at me with a huge grin. She reminds me of Quinn when we were younger, same brown hair and everything.

"Hello." I don't have a lot of experience with kids, so I don't really know what to say.

"Do you mind if we use your pool? I thought Hazel would enjoy swimming."

"Not at all; help yourself."

Mia grins at me. "Thank you!" She walks Hazel to one of the tables, and I find myself following them.

"Is he your boyfriend?" Hazel asks Mia, who looks a little flustered at the question. She glances in my direction.

"Well... he's a boy, and he's also my friend, so yes. Now, let's get some sunscreen on you before you swim. I'm not sending you back to your mom looking like a lobster." Hazel giggles as Mia rubs some lotion on her skin. I lower myself to sit in one of the chairs, inexplicably drawn to their interactions.

"Are you mad?" Hazel asks, eyeing me as Mia rubs lotion on her face. Mia shoots me an apologetic look, then turns her attention back to Hazel.

"He's not angry; he's just a little too serious. He doesn't laugh very much. Maybe you could try and get him to laugh today. You are the funniest person I know." Hazel giggles again. I didn't realize I looked angry, but I guess it doesn't surprise me. With all the shit that's going on in my brain, it makes sense that some of it would show on my face.

"Okay, you're all set! Let's let that soak in for a couple minutes before getting in the pool, okay? How about we just dip our toes in?" Mia pulls her shorts and tank top off to reveal a blue and teal swimsuit, which I have a hard time prying my eyes away from. It's a one-piece, with teal on the top, with wrapping up and over one shoulder. The teal blends into a deep blue on the bottom half, tightly hugging her curves. Mia catches me staring at her, and she waves me off with a shooing motion while her cheeks start to turn pink. They walk to the stairs of the pool, sit on the top step and set their feet in the water.

"John, will you come swimming with us? I can't cheer you up if you're all the way over there," Hazel calls to me.

I can't help but smile at her. She sure is cute. If only a little girl was all it took to get me out of my head.

"Sure thing, Hazel. I'll go put my suit on." She lights up, like I just told her I'd buy her a pony or something. By the time I come back, Mia and Hazel are splashing and swimming in the water. I cannon ball into the deep end, sending a wave of water splashing over both the girls. They both squeal and splash water back at me.

"Can I have a ride on your back, John? I'm not allowed in the deep end by myself yet." Her brown eyes look hopeful, and there's no way I can turn her down. I swim over to her, and she wraps her little arms around my back.

"You have a lot of muscles," she says, very matter of fact. Mia laughs; I take a deep breath and swim a few laps around the pool. On the third lap, I glance over at Mia, whose eyes are burning into mine.

"Look at you, Mr. Big Strong Army Man... swimming, making a sweet little girl's day," she calls out. Then she lowers her voice slightly, "I don't think I've ever been more attracted to you."

"Ew!" Hazel cries, and I chuckle.

We spend the next hour swimming, with Hazel showing us her diving skills in the shallow end. Then Mia goes inside to make us some sandwiches, while Hazel asks me a bunch of questions about surfing. She's never tried it, and I promise to teach her someday. I find myself a little bit disappointed when Julie calls Mia to say she's on her way to pick her up. I have to admit, Hazel has been a nice little distraction; I think I even got out of my head for a little bit today.

Hazel gives Mia a big hug goodbye, and then, to my surprise, she turns to me with her arms wide and flings herself at me. I crouch down just in time to catch her.

"I'm glad you're not mad anymore," she whispers. I give her a wink and pat the top of her head, not quite knowing what else to do. As we wave to her and Julie as they back out of the driveway, I feel Mia's arm slip around my waist.

"You were amazing with her! You didn't have to hang with us all day, but I'm sure glad you did. Do you know how hot you are when there's a cute kid on your shoulders?" she asks me, with a twinkle in her eyes.

I chuckle. "Easy now. I actually didn't mind it. She's fun to be around. And so are you." I lean down to kiss her on the cheek. She grins up at me, and then glances at her watch.

"Hey, I have a question," she says hesitantly. "I noticed that there are a couple bicycles in your garage?"

I nod. "Yeah, those were my aunt and uncle's... you want to go for a ride?"

Her face lights up. "Yes! I've been meaning to rent a bike but haven't gotten a chance yet. You could come with me, if you're up for it? Otherwise, I totally understand if you're sick of me, I can go by myself."

"I'm actually not sick of you." I say it in a matter of fact tone, and she laughs, but I really am surprised that I'd rather be with her than alone. "Let's go," I say, taking her hand in mine.

I wheel my aunt's bike over to Mia and quickly check the tire pressure before she climbs on. Once I do the same for my uncle's bike, we set off down the street.

"Where do you want to go?" I ask her.

"Doesn't really matter! We don't have to go through town... maybe just show me around some quieter parts of the island?"

"You got it."

For the next hour or so, I take her on a little tour of the Hawaii I knew as a kid. I make a big loop, stopping to show her the house I grew up in, and my elementary school. Matt's childhood home is near the school, so I show her that, too, as well as a park we used to play at.

When we come to the public beach access, we stop at one of the food trucks nearby to grab some fish tacos. It feels good to get some fresh air, but at the same time, all of these places just remind me of my old life and how nothing feels the same anymore. I feel disconnected, like all these memories are associated with someone else, and I'm just telling their story.

We eventually make our way back to the house, where I put the bikes back in the garage. When Mia grabs my hand, I wonder if she can tell something's off. Then again, everything's always off, so who knows what the hell she sees when she looks at me. I walk her to the cottage, and she wraps her arms around me in a hug.

"Thank you for today, for all of it," she whispers in my ear, sending a jolt of electricity through my body.

I kiss her softly. "You're welcome. Goodnight, Mia."

15

MIA

I start my day by filling my mug all the way to the top with coffee, right on the brink of overflowing. I'm going to need all of the caffeine I can get. After the amazing day yesterday with John and Hazel, I found it difficult to fall asleep. I couldn't stop my mind from racing, thinking about John and his struggles, and then to Julie and the challenges she must face being a single mom. I thought about Hazel, and wondered if she missed her dad at all, or if she had ever met him.

I have a tendency to be overly empathetic with the people I love, worrying and feeling the emotions right along with them. A side effect of being an emotional person, I suppose.

Eventually, I was able to quiet my thoughts and drift asleep, but I think I'm going to need caffeine reinforcements today. I make a plan to head to Julie's after I get back from my run. I pull a loose tank top over my sports bra and running shorts, and lace-up my running shoes.

When I step onto the sand, I decide to skip the run and just walk. I don't have the energy for a run today. I take a couple deep breaths to fill my lungs and exhale the air out as I leisurely make my way down the beach. After a few minutes, I feel a little bit more of a pep in my step. It feels good to move my body, and it's almost as if the sun is recharging my soul.

The beach isn't as busy this time of the day, and I only see a few people scattered on the sand. As I walk, I soak in the view— the stunning blue ocean jutting up to the cream-colored sand, the tall trees and greenery serving as the perfect accents for the landscape. There's a hint of light pink smeared across the sky, leftover from what must have been a killer sunrise.

I try and keep my mind clear as I walk, acknowledging any thoughts that I have, but then letting them go and bringing my mind back to a clear state. I learned this at a meditation retreat Paige and I went to a few years ago—I find it very helpful with stress management.

Eventually I turn around, heading back towards the cottage. After a quick shower, I grab my laptop and head to town. When I arrive at the coffee shop, I'm greeted with a smile from Julie, who looks significantly less stressed than yesterday.

"Hey!" she shoots me a grateful look. "Thanks again for yesterday. You're a lifesaver, Mia, seriously. What can I get you? Your usual? It's on the house."

"Oh, of course! It was my pleasure. Honestly, anytime!" I set my laptop bag on an empty table and have a seat. As I answer a few work emails, Julie walks over to deliver my drink.

"Here ya go." She smiles at me, setting the drink on the table. Then she grabs a water for herself and takes a seat next to me. "There's kind of a lull right now, mind if I sit for a minute? I'm exhausted."

"Of course!" I move my laptop over a few inches. "How's your sister doing?"

"She's doing all right. Her cast goes on today, I'll be taking her to the doctor over my lunch break. She's in a bit of pain, but overall doing well."

"I'm glad to hear that. Is Hazel at school?"

"Yup," she sighs as guilt washes over her face. "I love her to death, and I hate saying this out loud, but I kind of look forward to the days she's at school—it's so much easier to manage the coffee shop and get things done when she's taken care of somewhere else, you know?"

"I get it. It must be so challenging being a single mom, and doing everything on your own." I give her a sympathetic smile.

She nods in agreement. "You know, when her dad first left, I was so angry that it gave me fuel. I felt invincible, like I could handle anything without him. I was determined to prove that I didn't need him. But raising a child is nothing like what I expected. I'm just thankful I've had my family here to pitch in. And she's a great kid, which helps."

"When did her dad leave? Do you mind me asking?"

"Not at all. I met Hazel's dad, Mark, shortly after he moved here. He had come here on vacation and then decided to stay here full time and make a go at a food truck business." She sips her water and raises her eyebrows. "That's usually how it goes with tourists. They always come for the dream, wanting to live the vacation life all the time until reality smacks them in the face, and they realize that just because you live in paradise, that doesn't mean life's hardships just pass you by. A chilled margarita on the beach is amazing, but it's not enough to lessen the sting when life throws you a curveball—an unplanned pregnancy, in our case. He split as soon as I told him I was pregnant, haven't heard from him since."

"Oh wow. That must have been so hard. If it means anything, I think you've built a pretty great life for the two of you. She's an amazing little girl, you've raised her well. And you're running your own business—that's incredible, Julie!"

She smiles at me, taking a deep breath. "Thanks, Mia. I didn't mean to fish for praise. I'm doing alright, it's just nice to take a break every once in a while." She winks at me and puts her hand on my shoulder as she stands. "Let me know when you need a refill, okay?"

I smile and nod as I turn my attention back to work.

I've been working at Julie's for several hours when my phone buzzes with a text.

Paige: Call me when you get a chance to chat today!

I smile at my phone, and start packing up my things. Now seems like a good time to end the work day.

"Bye, Julie! Tell Hazel I say hi when you see her!" I call to Julie, who's in the middle of making what looks like a Frappuccino.

"Bye, Mia!" She waves me off with a grin.

Stepping outside, I'm hit with a wave of heat that washes over me, and I feel it all the way down to my toes. I slide my sunglasses on and pull my phone out to call Paige while I walk.

"Heyy, girlfriend!" she chirps in my ear.

"Hi, Paige! How are you?"

"I'm alright, you?"

"I'm great!"

"You want to hear about my disaster of a date last night?"

"Please."

"Okay, you know how Spencer's always trying to set me up with one of his high school friends? Well, I got sick of him hassling me, so I broke down and agreed to one date."

Walking up to a cute little tiki hut that overlooks the beach, I quietly order a lemonade. Then I walk onto the sand to sit on one of their chairs, all the while listening to Paige.

"So he set me up with his friend, Rob. Mia, I kid you not—it was the absolute worst date I have ever been on."

"Oh no! Why?"

"Let's just say he was more interested in his phone than he was in me. I met him at the restaurant, where he barely looked up long enough to even acknowledge me. He was too focused on his fantasy football stats to put in any effort. He asked me maybe one or two questions about myself throughout the entire meal, and when he did talk, he would just ramble on about his glory days playing football in high school. I had a longer conversation with our waiter."

"Ugh, that sucks. I'm sorry!"

"I didn't even stay to offer to pay for the bill. I had enough. I left before he was finished scarfing down his burger. What a waste of time. I swear, if I hear one more word from Spencer about setting me up, I'm gonna lose it. But on the plus side, the waiter was gorgeous and friendly, so the night wasn't a complete loss."

I snort. "Way to look on the bright side!"

"How are things going there?"

"Things are good! I watched Hazel yesterday for Julie, and then John and I went for a bike ride around the island."

"That sounds dreamy!"

"It really was."

"I know I say this every day, but I'm so jealous of you being there—I wish I could come back!"

I chuckle. "I know, I wish you could come back too! Too bad you can't teach from anywhere!"

"No kidding! Listen, I gotta run, I have some papers to grade before I head home. Call me tomorrow?"

"Sounds good, Bye Paige!"

I hang up and slide the phone into my bag. I sip the last few drops of my lemonade while gazing out at the ocean. Even though I came here under weird circumstances with Sean, I'm feeling extremely grateful for the time I have here, and I'm determined to make the most of it.

16

JOHN

"I don't have any charters booked for today, let's do it!" Brian offers when I call to ask if he'd take us fishing sometime. I'm caught off guard. I wasn't expecting him to be able to go *today*.

"Okay, great. Thanks, man."

"No problem. Meet me at the marina in an hour?"

"Sounds good."

I hang up and text Mia to make sure she still wants to go. When she texts back a "YES," I resign myself to the fact that I'm definitely going fishing today. I let out a deep breath, take a quick shower, throw some clothes on, and walk over to the cottage. I knock on the front door as I open it.

"Mia? You ready?" I call as I step inside the entryway.

"Yes! I just had to shower real quick after my run, but I'm ready now!" she replies, rushing to set her coffee cup in the sink, and snatching up her sunglasses.

"Is this what people wear fishing?" She holds her arms out

and looks up at me, and I push my lips together to hold my smile in, not wanting to laugh at her. She's wearing jean shorts and a white T-shirt that says *I LOVE TO FISH* across the front.

"I saw this in town this morning before my run... I wanted to be prepared." She pulls her ponytail through the hole in a baseball hat.

"You look stunning. Don't forget your sunglasses."

She grabs them again off the table and tucks one arm in the V of her T-shirt, and I remind myself to keep my eyes up.

As we drive to the marina, I can feel the nerves start to creep up. I shouldn't feel nervous. It's just Brian, and we're doing something I used to love, but it just doesn't feel right. I'm willing to try, though. Maybe going through the motions will somehow help my brain remember that this used to be second nature to me. We park, and I spot Brian's boat right away. I grab Mia's hand, wanting to feel stronger than I do. I thread my fingers through hers just as I feel my throat start to close up, and I swallow hard.

"John! My man! How's it goin'?" Brian calls out when he spots us approaching. I reluctantly release Mia's hand to shake his.

"Brian, this is Mia. Mia, Brian." He smiles at Mia.

"Nice to meet you, Mia." Turning back to me, he says, "I hope you don't mind; Matt kind of invited himself along. He should be here any minute." Before I can respond, Matt's voice booms behind us.

"Yo! John, what's up? Glad you finally want to go fishing. Mia, nice to see you again." He slaps me on the back and leans in to give Mia a kiss on the cheek. Matt is a natural flirt; I guess that's part of what makes him a great bartender. My jaw clenches, even though I realize I have no right to be jealous.

"I'm so excited, thanks for taking us out today," she tells Brian. We climb in the boat and set our stuff down while Brian finishes some last-minute prep.

"I brought some Dramamine if you want any. Do you get seasick?" I ask her.

"I don't think I do... I've been on a cruise ship before and I was fine, but I'm sure this might be different since it's a smaller boat. Maybe I'll take some just in case?"

"Probably a good idea. One tablet or two?"

"One's fine," she replies. I hand her a tablet and a bottle of water from Brian's cooler.

"All right, we ready? Let's get out there!" Brian starts up the boat, and we make our way through the channel until we're out on the open water. I sit with Mia on one of the benches on the side of the boat, hanging onto the rail to brace ourselves as the boat bobs up and down in the choppy waters. Once we're a couple miles offshore, we stop to catch some bait fish. Mia jumps right in, asking for guidance on what to do. Once we've got a couple of buckets of bait, we continue back out in the open water. Brian decides on a good spot about fifteen miles out, and we drop anchor and then start getting our lines ready.

For the next hour, I try to make a conscious effort to enjoy myself. I used to love fishing, and I'd like to try and figure out a way to enjoy it again. Besides, all I have to do is look at Mia —she makes me want to smile. In spite of the fact that fishing isn't her thing, she was so quick to offer to come with me. I know I wouldn't be nearly as relaxed if she weren't here next to me.

We each catch a few fish, mostly grouper and snapper. I get a small rush of excitement each time I feel the tug on the line, which is more than I expected. Brian manages to reel in a trophy Marlin, which he's pretty pumped about. Mia looks genuinely excited every time we reel a fish into the boat and insists on taking our picture with each one. She seems to get along with Matt and Brian well too, but that's one of the things I like about her—she can make a friend anywhere. I look out at the water and feel a small sense of peace. This is familiar, and there is something comforting about being out on the ocean without another boat in sight.

"You look good, man," Matt says next to me. We're at the bow, while Brian's in the back, showing Mia how to hook the bait fish. "Does Mia have anything to do with that?"

"What do you mean?"

"I'm just saying… you've barely ventured out of your house since you've been home, and then Mia shows up, and all of a sudden, you're at the bar fighting off drunk idiots, eating dinner with her at my restaurant, and now agreeing to go fishing after you turned me down how many times? I'm not busting your balls, man. I think it's a good thing. I think *she's* a good thing."

Not sure how to reply, I keep it simple. "I like her." He grins and slaps my back.

I've known Matt since grade school. His family moved to Hawaii in fourth grade, and he walked into the classroom like he owned the place. The teacher told him to sit in the seat next to mine, and he leaned over and asked if I wanted to play at his house or mine after school. I said mine, and we became instant friends. His confidence has always been alluring; people tend to gravitate to him. He's also got a mean right hook, which I discovered in high school when he caught me kissing one of his four sisters. I never made that mistake again. Needless to say, he's been a loyal friend to me, and even though I turn him down every time he asks me to do something, I appreciate that he keeps trying.

I glance back just in time to regret not giving Mia two Dramamine, because she's leaning over the side of the boat, dry heaving into the ocean.

Oh, shit.

Passing my rod off to Matt, I hurry to her side, grabbing one arm to make sure she doesn't lose her grip and go overboard.

"Are you okay?" I ask, and immediately want to punch myself in the face. *Of course, she's not alright!*

"Ughhhh," is the reply. She's still gripping the railing, and she leans her head down to rest on her arm.

"That's our cue to head back," says Brian. He and Matt reel in all of the lines and secure all of the latches while I tend to Mia. I grab a Sea Band from Brian's bag and slide it on her wrist, then move her to the middle of the back of the boat, assuming that will be the best place for her to sit. She puts her head in her hands, and I keep my hand on her back the whole ride back to shore, brushing my thumb back and forth.

As the boat slows down and we're getting closer to the marina, the water gets choppy and Mia throws up again over the back of the boat. When the boat comes to a stop, Brian and Matt wave us off, saying they'll deal with cleaning things up.

Once back on land, Mia staggers a bit and attempts to wave to the guys as she keeps her eyes pressed shut. I grab her waist, pull her arm around my shoulder, and help her walk back to the car.

"You really don't have to do this," Mia tells me as I help her lie down and pull the covers over her. She lies on her back, eyes still closed, and she raises her hands to her forehead.

"Is it normal to still feel like I'm on a boat? Like the world is still moving?"

"Yeah, that's normal," I tell her regretfully as I sit on the side of the bed.

"I'm so sorry, John. I feel so bad. Today was a big deal for you, and I went and ruined it by puking everywhere. If I hadn't gotten sick, you would still be out there."

"Don't apologize. There's nowhere else I'd rather be." It's true. Screw fishing... as much fun as it was today, it was only that enjoyable for me because Mia was there.

"Please apologize to Brian and Matt for me."

"I will... you did that several times already, though." I hand her a cracker, and she takes a tiny nibble.

"Ugh. Will you talk to me? It'll take my mind off being nauseous."

I think for a second, and then say the thing that's been on the tip of my tongue for the past couple days. "Um, well, I'm just throwing this out there, but... nobody's booked the cottage after you. It'll be empty for three weeks after you leave. Just letting you know in case you were interested in extending your stay."

Her eyes fly open, search immediately for mine, and then she moans, shakes her head and closes them again.

"Just think about it. No pressure."

Her lips curve up into a small smile, eyes still closed, "I knew you liked me."

I chuckle. I grab her hand and stare at her, taking advantage of her closed eyes. I've never considered myself a lucky person, but I just might be changing my mind. I wonder how I got so lucky that out of all the Airbnbs in Hawaii, she chose mine.

"Yes, you did."

17

MIA

Mia: Book me for three more weeks, please.

The very first thing I did after waking up was call my boss and get her approval for working remotely for a bit longer. I know it's a little bit crazy, changing my plans for a guy I've known for just a few weeks, especially since I will eventually be going back to Minnesota. There's no getting around that. But, I'm not ready to say goodbye to John just yet. I haven't felt a connection like this with someone in my entire life, and I want to spend more time with him.

More importantly, my presence seems to be good for him. I can see his walls slowly coming down. It may be at a turtle's pace, but who am I to push? I have no idea what's going on in his mind, or what he went through overseas. There's no way that I want to leave when he's just starting to make progress. I like being the person that eases some of his pain.

John: You got it. :) What are you up to today?

My first thought is to head into town and grab a coffee from Julie before stopping in the bookstore. However, I feel like I'm getting a good read on John, and I know he would be more comfortable at the beach. Baby steps.

Mia: Will you teach me to surf? Or at least attempt to?

John: I can do that. Meet you outside in thirty min?

Mia: See ya then!

I get myself ready and meet him in his garage, where he's pulling his surfboard off the wall.

"You do know what you got yourself into, right?" I ask John on our way to the beach. "I've never surfed a day in my life."

"Well, it can't be as bad as fishing," he teases. "But we'll practice on the sand first." He shoots me a smile. "So you decided to stay, huh?"

"Yeah… I mean, why wouldn't I want to? I'm in Hawaii, for Pete's sake. Who wouldn't want to stay longer in paradise? It definitely has nothing to do with a guy. Absolutely nothing," I tease him back. I can feel him watching me, and I turn to see the corner of his mouth turn up into a smirk.

"I like when you smile," I say softly, looking back down at the ground.

"I like when you make me smile," he answers, sending butterflies into a tailspin in my stomach.

"Thanks again for taking care of me yesterday. Now I know that I definitely do get seasick. Next time I'll take two Dramamine."

"You would go again after that?" He seems surprised.

"Sure... what's a little vomit? Besides, you looked like you were actually enjoying yourself."

"I was."

We reach an open stretch of sand, and John sets the board down. I'm glad to find that it's not too busy by our spot on the beach... for John's sake and for mine. I can pretty much predict how this is going to go, and it's not gonna be pretty. I drop my phone and sunglasses on my towel and take a deep breath, clapping my hands together.

"All right, show me what ya got, teacher."

We spend the next half-hour practicing with me laying down, pretending to paddle, and then jumping up into position to surf the wave. I am sweating in no time, and my thighs are on fire. No wonder surfers are always in such good shape; it's quite the workout.

"Okay, you ready to try it in the water?"

My heart starts to race, and nerves take over. Wanting to show him that I can step outside of my comfort zone, too, I try to put on a brave face.

"Let's do it," I reply, probably not as convincingly as I imagine. I tug my shorts and tank top off, even more sure I made the right choice by going with my black one-piece instead of a bikini. At least I'll have a fighting chance of keeping my lady parts covered when a wave inevitably knocks me over.

He leads me into the water, where I climb on the board and lay on my stomach. He pushes the board while I paddle out a ways and then manage to turn it around, facing the shore.

"John, don't let go," I say, mildly panicking.

"I'm right here. Here comes a wave. When I say 'now,' you jump up to surfing stance, okay? You ready?"

"Okay..."

When John yells for me to hop up, my body refuses, and I cling tighter to the sides of the board, letting the wave wash over me.

"What the hell was that?" John says with a laugh, swimming over to rescue me and the board I'm still firmly attached to.

"I couldn't do it!" I whine.

"I see that. Do you want to try again?"

"I suppose…"

I wish I could say the next few attempts are better, but they most definitely are not. I do attempt to stand up, but get knocked down over and over again, until I finally call it quits. Completely out of breath, I stumble onto the beach and flop down on my back, not even caring that I'm not on a towel. John sets the board down and lays down next to me.

"Oh my gosh, I'm gonna be so sore tomorrow," I say, panting.

John rolls onto his side, facing me, propping his head up with his hand. "You did better than I thought you were gonna do, honestly."

I smack his chest, and he snickers. "Shut up."

"No, seriously, I'm impressed. A lot of people would have given up after the first try, but you kept going. I'm proud of you."

I turn my head to face him, the sand crunching under my hair. "Yeah?"

"Yeah."

I expect him to give me a warm smile, but what I get instead is a heated stare that grows stronger by the second. My heart is already beating hard from the surfing disaster, but it starts racing even faster as he leans in and presses his lips to mine. He scoots closer until his body is resting against my side, his sandy arm sliding around my waist. I kiss him back, putting my hand on his arm and angling myself so I can press into him.

We stay this way, lost in absolute bliss, until we hear a cat call coming from somewhere on the beach. We separate and quietly laugh, suddenly remembering that we're in public. His eyes still burn into mine, still so intense. He clears his throat.

"You ready to head back?" His voice is gravelly.

"Yeah," I say with a nod. "I have sand everywhere, and I need to shower. Why don't you come to the cottage? We can get cleaned up, and I'll make us something for dinner while you're in the shower."

He offers me a hand to help me to my feet. "Sounds great." He tucks his board under one arm, and me under the other. We walk back in silence, covered head to toe in sand.

I place our sandwiches on a plate, and finish cutting the honeydew into a bowl. There is an article spread out on the kitchen table that I had printed out earlier for work, so instead of organizing and moving it out of the way, I opt to pull myself up to sit on the counter next to the sink. I pop a honeydew piece in my mouth, trying to ignore the fact that John is in my bathroom, taking a shower, most likely without any clothes on. No, *definitely* without any clothes on. I pick up my phone to text Paige. I am in desperate need of a distraction.

Mia: How's it going?

Luckily it doesn't take her too long to answer.

Paige: Oh, you know, just living the dream, trying not to freeze to death. How are things there? How's John?

Mia: John's good. He tried to teach me how to surf today.

Paige: Omg I would have loved to witness that… break any bones?

Mia: No, I did excellent, thank you very much. I'm a natural.

Details, details.

Paige: Yeah, right… I can't believe you're staying even longer, I need my best friend back!

Mia: I'll be home before you know it. We can freeze together.

Paige: Did you see Kelly's Instagram post? She's pregnant! Due in August.

I'm thrilled, but Kelly and her new baby are gonna have to wait, because the door to the bathroom opens, and John comes out. He's wearing a pair of shorts we grabbed on our way back. Apparently, he keeps a couple extra shorts and shirts in his outdoor closet by the pool just in case he needs them. He must have something against shirts, though, because he's not wearing one.

So much for trying to be distracted—my focus zeroes right back in on John, specifically on how mesmerizing he is without a shirt on. Miles of tanned, smooth skin. I set my phone down on the counter and watch him. His brown hair is a ruffled mess on top of his head, still wet from the shower. His skin is golden brown, with a hint of red from the sun today. He crosses the room and stands next to me, grabbing a sandwich.

"Thanks for making these. I'm starving. Surfing really works up an appetite, doesn't it?"

"Sure does. Especially when you suck at it." I offer him a smile and a piece of honeydew.

"No papaya tonight?"

"Just trying to have a little variety."

He pops it in his mouth and grabs us a couple beers from the fridge. He opens both then, handing one to me, and taking a sip of the other.

"Thanks again for today. You were a very patient teacher," I tell him.

"No problem." He shoots me a warm smile, which I focus on, and all of a sudden, I'm not hungry anymore. His smile does something to me, especially because I know he doesn't give it out to just anyone.

"You know... if you keep kissing me like that, on the beach... I might never go home," I tell him. Something shifts in his eyes, and his mouth lifts up into a smirk.

"Oh yeah? That's all it would take, huh?" He moves closer, until he's standing right in between my legs. When I'm sitting on the counter like this, we're the same height, so my eyes stare directly into his, which are growing darker by the second. I smile at him and bring my hands to rest on his shoulders, mentally willing him to come closer. He must be telepathic because he brings his face forward to kiss me. My legs brush against the sides of his hips, and I run my hands back to rest around his neck. He brings his hands to my waist and pushes himself against me, causing me to let out a small gasp.

Oh boy, I'm in trouble.

He breaks away to place a kiss right below my ear, slowly moving down my neck.

"Do you do this with all your tenants?" I tease.

His chuckle vibrates against my neck. "No, you're just special."

Good answer.

I grab his face with my hands and pull him up to look into my eyes. "How special?" He must pick up on the challenge in my voice, because the next thing I know, his hands slide under my butt, and he lifts me up. I squeal and wrap my legs around his waist. We make our way down the hall, lips pressed together, until we reach my bedroom—where he proves to me just how special he thinks I am.

18

JOHN

I wake up with one of Mia's arms draped across my chest, and her leg bent at the knee on top of mine. I don't want to wake her, so I lay there quietly. My mind starts drifting. Last night was absolutely incredible. I felt so connected to Mia it was almost overwhelming. I was nervous that it might be too much for me, but there was no way in hell I could stop once she gave me the green light. A part of me hopes it wasn't a mistake. I had been hesitant to stay the night, worried I might have a night terror. It's been a few weeks since my last one, and I never know when it's gonna happen. Ultimately, I couldn't bring myself to leave her. I'm glad I stayed, and I remind myself to not overthink or stress about it.

Mia stirs next to me and stretches, slowly opening her eyes. I smile at her when her eyes find mine. She curls onto her side, facing me. Her blonde hair is a wavy mess surrounding her face, and she has never looked more beautiful.

"I like waking up next to you," I tell her.

"Me too," she replies with a lazy smile.

I shift onto my side and prop my elbow up on the pillow. "What do you have planned today?"

She runs a hand through her hair as she thinks. "I do need to go into town and pick up some groceries. Probably stop and see Julie and Hazel. I might bring my laptop; I actually have a lot of work to get done today." She looks at me regretfully. "Is that okay? I don't want you to feel used after last night, that I got what I needed, and now I'm kicking you to the curb..." She says all this with a smirk, so I know she's kidding.

I grin back at her and tickle her side until she's squirming and begging me to stop. "I see how it is... no, it's all good. I have some stuff I need to get done today too. Probably go check on Rose. Do you want to meet later for dinner? Maybe a picnic on the beach?"

Her eyes light up. "Oh, that sounds amazing! Yes, let's do that!"

We stare at each other for a few minutes, neither one of us wanting to break the spell. I like this little bubble we're in, and I would be just fine if we never left. It's easier to forget everything else and just focus on Mia. Eventually, we climb out of bed, and I pull on my shorts from last night while she walks naked to the bathroom, me staring shamelessly. In the kitchen, I make her a bowl of cereal with milk, and place it on the counter right as she ventures into the room.

"Oh, thanks!" She picks up the bowl and scoops a spoonful into her mouth.

"You're welcome." I walk towards her, place my hand on her low back, and kiss her cheek. "I'll see you later. Let me know when you're ready for dinner."

"I will," she says softly, watching me as I head for the door. When I glance back, she's still watching me, eating her cereal. She gives me a smile before I close the door.

I walk back to the main house, allowing myself to feel the happiness that's tugging at my chest. It takes a conscious effort to remind myself that it's okay to let the good things in. Mia makes me happy, and she seems to be somehow helping me get to a better place. Who knows what's going to happen when she eventually goes back home, but I might as well let her in as much as I can while she's here. When she leaves, at least she would be leaving me a less broken man than I was before.

After I shower and do my pool chores, I spend the rest of the day at Rose's, helping her with some computer stuff and organizing her mail. Typically Rose and I don't talk very much —it's one of the reasons I like her—but today, she seems to have a million things on her mind.

"You know, I met that cute young lady staying in your cottage. Mia, is it? She sure is a peach. Good looking, too!"

"She is." I'm trying not to encourage her, so I keep my tone neutral.

"I've seen the two of you walking to the beach several times now. It's nice that she keeps you company. You must get lonely over there all by yourself."

"I do just fine," I reply, not wanting to give Rose what she wants, which is gossip.

I manage to tune her out and finish what I came here to do.

"Bye, Rose," I call out as I leave, instead of my usual wave goodbye.

"Bye, John. Thank you for your help, as always."

I hop in my car back at my house and run into town to pick up some food for our picnic. I know it's only been a few hours since I've seen her, but it's been a few hours too long. On my way back, Mia texts that she'll be ready in twenty minutes.

Back at the house, I set our containers of food from town in the picnic basket. I wasn't even aware I had a picnic basket here until I looked in the closet in the laundry room. My aunt must have left it for me. Shows how much I pay attention, I guess. The door by the patio slides open, and Mia steps inside.

"Hey!" She walks to me and slips her arm around me. "How are you?" Wrapping my arms around her in a hug, I feel a sense of calm wash over me. I don't know how to explain what happens to me when she's around. All I know is I feel instinctively drawn to her. I feel a glimmer of hope for actual happiness when I'm with her.

"I'm so excited to go to the beach; I've been inside for most of the day, and I need some fresh air!" She's wearing jean shorts and a loose gray tank top. Her blonde hair is down and wavy. I'm just about to grab the basket when my phone rings on the counter. Quinn's name lights up the screen.

"Oohh! Is that your sister?" Mia's eyebrows lift up in excitement.

"Yeah… I'll just call her later." I bring the phone to my pocket, but Mia's hand stops me.

"Oh no! Don't not answer because of me. Go ahead, pretend I'm not even here!"

Reluctantly, I answer the phone.

"Hey, Quinn."

"Hey John, how's it going?"

"Fine. You?"

"Amazing. Guess what I did yesterday?" I don't even respond, just wait for her to continue. "Some friends and I went on a tour of Matanuska Glacier… coolest thing ever. They gave us ice cleats, and we explored the whole thing on foot. It was absolutely breathtaking!" Apparently Quinn's voice is loud enough for Mia to hear, because Mia's eyes widen, and she lets out a "so cool!" I know she meant for it to be just for me, but my sister instantly picks up on it.

"Who is that? Jonathan! Do you have a woman with you?" she asks pointedly. I sigh, realizing there's no point in lying to her.

"Yes."

"Can I speak to her?"

I glance at Mia, who's clapping her hands together and nodding. I hand her the phone with a shake of my head.

"Quinn? Hi, I'm Mia. It's so nice to talk to you!" she says. "I'm renting the cottage from John... uh-huh... yes... he's doing good, we're about to go to the beach for a picnic." When I realize this probably won't be a short conversation, I lean my elbows against the kitchen counter to wait. They talk for about ten more minutes, which doesn't surprise me. They both like to talk, and Lord knows Mia's never met a stranger. "Of course. All right, sounds good! Bye!" She hangs up and hands me the phone with a smile. "She says bye." I can't help but smile at her. I actually don't mind that she hijacked my phone call; it saved me from having to dodge all of the questions that Quinn usually has for me. I put my phone in my pocket and grab the basket of food.

"Okay, I've got the food and a couple of towels. Ready?"

She nods, and we start our walk to the beach. On the way, we talk—really Mia talks—about what she did today.

"So I went to Julie's coffee shop this morning to work, and I made the mistake of sitting at the table right next to Hazel." She laughs. "Gosh, she is so cute. She would not stop talking. She told me all about all of her friends at school. I'm not kidding— each and every one. I hardly got any work done... then I grabbed some groceries. Oh! I grabbed some burgers if you want to grill sometime this week... oh! And *then* I found this adorable little touristy shop along the main strip in town—" She stops abruptly and looks at me sheepishly.

"Sorry... I'm a rambler. Sometimes I have to remind myself to stop talking."

I'm actually surprised that I don't find her rambling overwhelming. Usually, it's hard to cut through the fog and focus enough to follow along when people are talking fast, but once again, everything is different with Mia. I shake my head and grab her hand. "Don't change who you are. I like that you're chatty. I like everything about you."

She blushes and smiles, squeezing my hand. We find a spot to sit on the sand, lay the towels out next to each other, and set the picnic basket on top. I pull the food containers out, open them, and set them down with the silverware. Since I know she enjoyed the ahi tuna when we had that; I picked us up some poke bowls. Poke is a popular Hawaiian food made of raw fish—I chose ahi tuna this time. I also grabbed some green beans and short ribs in case she wasn't in the mood for raw fish.

"Oh, you brought wine!" She pulls out a bottle of chardonnay that I brought, as well as the ten-ounce stainless steel tumblers I thought would be perfect for the wine. She opens the bottle and pours some into the tumblers. She sits cross-legged on the towel, and I lay on my side, propped up on my elbow. We eat in silence, enjoying the view, listening to the waves crash onto the shore. After we finish eating and put the empty food containers back in the basket, I sit back down and pat the sand in front of me, motioning for her to sit down. She climbs in between my legs, scooching back until her back is pressed against my chest. She rests her elbows on my knees, which are slightly bent.

"This is nice," she says, laying her head back to rest against my shoulder. I wrap my arms around her, and I feel like I could stay this way for the rest of my life and not want to move. I kiss her temple, and she twists her head around to kiss me on the lips, sending a wave of warmth through me that I realize I'm starting to crave. We sit like that, taking sips of our wine and watching as the sun finally starts to set.

"Wow, it's so beautiful," she whispers.

"It is… just like you."

"Oh, don't get cheesy on me now," she teases me, and I laugh, squeezing her tighter. We stay there until the sun is no longer visible on the horizon, then quietly gather our stuff and walk back to the cottage, hand in hand.

19

JOHN

"John... John, wake up!" I hear Mia's muffled voice from far away. *Mia?* My shoulder moves back and forth as if someone's shaking it. "John, wake up!" Mia's panicked voice gets louder, and the shaking gets more real as I'm pulled from my dream. I shout as I sit up, coming back to reality. My heart is pounding in my chest, and I can't seem to catch my breath. *Fuck.* I look around, searching for any small detail to focus on to help calm myself down.

Where am I?

I'm in Mia's bed... in the cottage... drenched in sweat, my body shaking uncontrollably. Mia's hand touches my arm, and I jump at the contact. I swallow hard, trying to keep my throat from closing.

I need air.

I stumble out of the bed and move down the hallway, slamming into the wall as I go. Opening the front door, I sit down on the top step of the stairs, put my head in my hands, and focus on taking as deep of breaths as I can. I zero in on the smell of the air, the color of the leaves on the trees, and the buzzing of the street lights. After a few moments, my heart starts to slow down, and my head clears. I spend a few minutes breathing in and out, my body not ready to move yet.

The door opens behind me. "John? You all right?" Mia cautiously peeks her head out. I turn to face her. She looks terrified, and I hate that I scared her.

"I'm okay. I'm sorry… I just need a minute, okay?"

She nods. "I'm right inside if you need anything." She quietly shuts the door. I exhale out a deep breath. I hate that she saw me like this, that I had a night terror right next to her. God only knows what I had said out loud. I shake my head, feeling discouraged and embarrassed. Even though my body is relatively back to normal now—whatever normal means—my mind is still wired. I think back to the events that triggered the night terror. The events that trigger them all…

7 months earlier
Iraq

The sound of a twig breaking under my boot echoes through the trees. The hair on the back of my neck stands up as I clutch my rifle and scan my eyes over the brush for anything out of place.

My platoon, which consists of about twenty-five soldiers, is conducting a daily perimeter check that's taking us down the left side of the mountain. We perform this mission every single day, and every single day it has the same effect of scaring me shitless.

Private Connor Roach, who's been my buddy since basic training, is about eight people ahead of me, right behind Private

Luis Garcia, who I also consider a good friend. Not that I don't consider every single one of these guys my brothers, cause I do. Roach and Garcia are just the ones I've spent the most down time with. We've become super close.

Our cots are next to each other back at base camp, and we've spent many sleepless nights talking about our lives back home and where we grew up. You can learn a lot about someone if you're desperate enough to take your mind away from wherever you are.

We continue down the trail, all of our senses heightened and on guard. All of a sudden, a bullet whizzes between Myer and Rodriguez, missing Myer by about 3 inches.

Fuck. Fuck. Fuck.

We all take cover as best we can. I crouch behind a nearby tree, rifle raised and pointed in the direction of where the bullet came. Mere seconds later, another bullet whizzes through the trees. Luckily it doesn't make contact with anyone, but unluckily, that's when I notice helmets rising up out of the brush ahead of us. Those helmets are fastened to about forty enemy heads, whose rifles are pointed right at us.

Shit.

They easily outnumber us. Blood pumps through my veins as adrenaline kicks into high gear. Sergeant Cooper calls out, "Stand your ground! Hanson, radio for air support now! We need drone assistance ASAP!" Adam Hanson was our signaller—he always traveled with a radio and was our point of contact for field communication.

Hanson is a few feet from me, and I hear him radio in coordinates for a drone strike, but my eyes stay glued to the enemy. It would only be a few minutes while we wait for the drone, but unfortunately, it looks like we'll have a fight on our hands while we wait. More gunfire rings through the trees, and I hear an anguished scream from somewhere on my right, then,

"We need a medic!" I join my fellow soldiers in returning fire, holding our position.

I didn't think I could possibly be any more scared, but I was wrong—fear and panic become absolutely paralyzing when I realize they're starting to advance toward us. It's at that moment the missiles from the drone come flying down and connect with the group of enemies, sending bodies flying.

"Hanson! Another drone strike!" Sergeant Cooper yells. Hanson relays another set of coordinates into his radio, his voice shaky with adrenaline.

This was the moment that none of us would ever forget, because Hanson's heartbreaking mistake would not only come with grave consequences—it was also the one thing I haven't been able to forgive him for.

Somehow, he is off on his coordinates by eighty feet, missing the mark. Instead of hitting the enemies, the missiles come into contact with a line of bushes that are on the outskirts of our position. As it hits the ground, it also takes out four of our own men.

Fuuuuck.

My body shifts into auto-pilot and keeps returning fire. My brain won't allow me to process it until much later, once backup arrives, and we make it to safety. It is then that I learn two of the four soldiers killed are Roach and Garcia.

I don't allow myself to think about what happened very often. There is absolutely no hope of keeping my head above water if I constantly live in that memory. It is a big reason why I can't bring myself to talk to Adam. I know I shouldn't blame him; it was a mistake, and I know he is extremely remorseful about it. From what I've heard, he hasn't been dealing with it well. But how can I extend a life raft to someone else if all I have is the raft I'm on and it's barely keeping me afloat?

I let out a shaky breath and wipe the tears that fell from my eyes. I push the memory down, just like I do every single day, and open the door to head back inside the cottage. I need Mia. I know I won't be able to sleep anymore tonight, but I know without a doubt that I need to be close to her.

I walk into the bedroom and crawl in the bed, sliding over to put my arm around Mia, who is curled up on her side facing the other way. I push into her until every part of my body is touching hers. She lays her arm gently over the top of my arm that's pressed against her stomach.

"I didn't know what to do... you were screaming and shaking, so I wanted to wake you up—was that okay? I'm sorry if that wasn't the right thing to do," she says quietly.

"It's fine... I'm sorry," I whisper.

"What happened? What were you dreaming about?"

"Mia... I can't." If I can hardly allow myself to think about it, how am I supposed to talk about it?

She nods, and we spend the rest of the night not moving from each other. Mia eventually falls asleep, but I am wide awake, wondering how the hell this was fair to her. When the clock finally reads 5:45 a.m., I kiss Mia's temple and quietly slip out of the bed. I feel guilty that she had to experience that, and I hate that it's something that I can't control. Maybe this whole thing is a bad idea. She's supposed to be on vacation and enjoying herself, not worrying about me and my baggage. I quietly grab my things and walk out of the cottage, needing to be alone.

20

MIA

It's been a weird couple days. After John had his night terror—which scared the hell out of me, by the way—he's been in a funk. I can feel him shutting down and putting up a wall again. I wish it was easier for him to open up to me; then I would know how to be there for him. I feel useless most of the time, not knowing what to do. We've slept in the same bed together every night, and I get the feeling he doesn't like to sleep alone. But during the day, he's been avoiding eye contact with me and doesn't smile as much as he used to. His face has gone back to being stoney and hard.

Tonight I have a plan to hopefully lighten the mood a little bit. I made us a huge salad for dinner, and I bring that and a bottle of wine over to the backyard patio by the pool. I'm wearing a cute white floral sundress, and curled my hair. I set the salad on a table and then open the sliding door.

"John? I'm here!" I call into the quiet house.

He appears in the hallway and gives me a tight smile. To his credit, I can see how much he's trying. It's like he's going through the motions, but the light's just not on inside. He's wearing jeans and a light blue polo shirt, which reminds me that he looks absolutely striking in blue. He comes closer and kisses my cheek as he walks past me outside.

"Come sit down! I made us dinner," I say cheerfully, gesturing to the table I moved next to the pool.

"This looks great. Thank you." Even his voice is slightly flat.

As we eat, I tell him about my day, trying to get him to react to anything I'm saying. He nods every once in a while, but he's just not here, not present with me tonight. My stomach starts to sink a little bit. What if I can't get through to him? What if he wants nothing to do with me anymore?

After we finish eating, I push my chair back, stand up, and move to stand next to his chair, offering him my hand. "Come on, I want to dance with you," I whisper.

"Dance with me?" He looks at me, brows furrowed in confusion. "I don't have music out here."

"I've taken care of that." I use my phone to turn on music that is connected to the wireless speaker I bought in town and placed on the ground by the house. "Perfect" by Ed Sheeran starts playing through the speakers. I look into his eyes, maintain eye contact, and pull him up to stand. We walk a few feet away from the table, and I bring his hands around to rest on my lower back. I put my arms around the top of his shoulders, and we start swaying to the slow beat. I take a deep breath and savor his scent. He smells woodsy, with hints of cedar and spice. There's also a hint of salt. I suspect most guys born and raised in Hawaii smell a little bit like the ocean.

I refuse to take my eyes from his, hoping that he'll find whatever it is he's searching for in mine. I run my hands from his shoulders down his arms and back up again. His eyes still locked on mine, his face starts to slowly soften, and I see a glimpse of

John coming back. The fog in his eyes is clearing, and I can finally recognize the man who's staring back at me. Relief floods over me.

There you are.

I bring my hands to his neck and let out a sigh. "John... I know I can't even begin to understand what you're going through, but I want to help you any way I can. I just wish I knew how to be there for you."

His eyes look regretful, and he hesitates, struggling with what to say. "It's not you at all, Mia. You help me so much by just being here, you have no idea. I just... there's things I can't get past... I... I just don't know how to deal sometimes... and I don't want to drag you down with me."

I shake my head. "I'm a big girl, John. If I didn't think I could handle it, I wouldn't even try. I'm not scared of this." I let a few seconds pass in silence. "Have you thought about seeing someone? A therapist? There are resources available for you, right?" I ask hesitantly, nervous about what his reaction will be.

His face hardens, and he blows out a breath. "I haven't been able to work up the nerve to do it. I'm terrified of going down that road. The thought of reliving it all makes me sick to my stomach."

I nod softly, my heart breaking for him. "That's understandable." I push my lips together in a sympathetic smile. "Thanks for being honest with me." I don't want to push the issue, so I smile at him again, wanting to lift the mood. "Well, I'm here if you ever want to talk or anything. I'll be there for you in any way I can. I kinda like you, you know."

He finally gives me the warm smile that I've missed the last couple days. "I like you, too," he says and leans down to kiss my lips. As soon as his lips touch mine, I hang onto him tighter and push into him, refusing to let him pull back. He parts his lips and kisses me with such intensity my knees start to go weak. He grips my waist tighter, gathering the fabric of my dress in his hands, and pulling me further into him. He eventually breaks the kiss, but doesn't let me go.

"I'm sorry I've been distant the last couple days... this is why It's not fair to—"

I cut him off. "Let's go swimming." I grab his hand and tug him towards the pool.

"Right now? We're dressed..." He's looking at me like I'm crazy. Maybe I am? Maybe I am absolutely out of my mind for him.

"So what? Carpe Diem, John... let's live in the moment. Get out of your head and come swimming with me." I'm almost to the edge, my back to the pool, facing John.

He slowly grins, and next thing I know, he's charging at me, grabbing me by the hips and pushing us both in the pool. I squeal and grip his shoulders as we go under the water. Surfacing, I gasp for a breath and let out a laugh.

"Okay, maybe swimming in this dress wasn't the best idea," I say, panting. I'm struggling to push my legs far enough apart to tread water. John comes to my rescue, his strong arm coming beneath my knees to carry me sideways to shallower water. He sets me down once I can touch.

"Thank you, kind sir."

"You know, I don't think I've ever been in this pool with this many clothes on," John muses, swimming around me. "Without clothes, on the other hand..." He turns to me and winks, to which I respond with a smile.

"Did you swim here a lot growing up?"

"Yeah, the house I grew up in didn't have a pool, and my parents were pretty close to my aunt and uncle, so we were over here all the time."

"Why did your aunt and uncle move?"

"For work. My uncle's job offered him a big pay raise to transfer to their corporate office in Cali. They moved while I was overseas, but they came back when I got home to help me get settled in the house."

"Do you like living here?"

"I do, for the most part... I definitely wouldn't be able to afford this on my own."

I nod and lean back to float, doing bird flaps. John leans against the pool wall, watching me.

"You know, chlorine is terrible for my hair. It dries it out like crazy... you should consider yourself pretty lucky; I don't risk damaging my hair for just anybody," I tease. Still floating, I shift my eyes to the side and find John smiling. My heart sighs in relief, because damn is it good to see him smile.

He comes closer, places a hand under my back to help keep me afloat, and leans down to give me a gentle kiss. "How do you somehow always know exactly what I need?" he asks softly. I smile up at him, and we spend the rest of the evening floating under the stars. As grateful as I am for being able to lessen some of John's pain tonight, I find myself desperately wishing I knew how to take it all away for good.

When we're done swimming, John brings me out a T-shirt and boxers of his to wear while we clear the table and wash the dishes in the kitchen. Once everything's put away, John turns to me. "Do you want to sleep here or at the cottage?" We've slept here at the main house a couple of times so far, but we mostly sleep at the cottage. There's something about that place. It's small and quaint, which makes it seem that much cozier and feels like we're living in our own little world over there. I've quickly fallen in love with it.

"Cottage? I didn't bring my toothbrush or anything over."

"Sounds good." He turns off all the lights in the main house and locks the pool door. We walk to the cottage by moonlight, and I grab John's hand, feeling pretty good about the evening. John definitely seems lighter, and that makes me happy.

Once inside, I change into my pajama tank and shorts, then head to the bathroom to brush my teeth. As I'm brushing, John appears wearing just his pants. He knows I can't resist him when he's shirtless. He comes up behind me, bringing his head down to kiss the spot where my neck meets my shoulder. A shiver runs through me as he gently slides the strap of my tank top down to trail more kisses along my skin. I lean my head in the opposite direction to give him more room while his other arm comes around, and he rests his hand flat on my stomach, gently pushing me back into him. I'm not sure why my mind chooses this moment to wander, but I find myself wondering if I should be nervous or scared of him. Would other girls be hesitant to get involved with someone who clearly has some mental shit they were working through? Maybe... but I just can't see a single thing that would scare me off with John. I don't see danger when I look into his eyes. I just see devastation and heartbreak.

I finish brushing, rinse, and set my toothbrush on the counter. I slowly turn, while he keeps his body pressed against mine, slip my arms around his waist, tucking my fingers into the pants near the top of his butt. I lean forward and plant a kiss right in the middle of his chest, then look up just in time to connect with John's mouth that is moving down toward me. We kiss for a few minutes, each second increasing the urgency I'm certain we both feel. I bring my hands to his chest and push against him until he starts to slowly move. I back him out of the bathroom, and veer him left down the hall to the bedroom. We never break our kiss, even as we enter the room, and he spins me around, slamming the door shut with his foot.

21

MIA

"Do you love him?" Paige's voice asks from my phone. I have her on speaker on the kitchen table so I can type on my laptop at the same time.

"I mean, I'm definitely falling for him. I like him a lot, Paige. A lot. I've never felt a connection like this with anyone else. But at the same time, it's hard to be in love with someone who's holding back and not giving you one hundred percent, you know? We're definitely not completely there yet."

"So you're supposed to come home, when? Two weeks? Have you guys talked about what'll happen once you leave?"

I came clean with Paige this morning, telling her the truth about how we were just pretending at first, but then eventually naturally fell for each other. She was hurt that I had lied to her, which I still feel bad about, but she wasn't surprised that John and I are a thing now. She said it was obvious that we had chemistry.

It's been about a week since my cheer-up attempt at the main house. It seemed to work, and we've actually had a really great week. We've been to the beach so John can surf a few times. He's offered to teach me again, but so far, I haven't taken him up on it. I'm trying to build up the courage to try again.

When I mentioned that I'd like to go snorkeling, he took me to this secluded cove that he grew up going to. It wasn't crowded at all—apparently, it's a spot that only locals know about, and there's an unspoken rule that nobody tells the tourists about it. It felt good to be let in on the secret. It was absolutely breathtaking, definitely one of my favorite days in Hawaii so far. While I was holding John's hand, snorkeling and watching all of the marine life, I felt so incredibly happy I thought I might burst.

I even convinced him to come have dinner with me in town again, on a weekday, of course, and then we stopped to see Matt at the bar on the way home. It's been really amazing. I've been able to see a glimpse of what life with John could really be like, and I'm not going to lie—it looks really good.

"No, we haven't talked about it. We're both avoiding that topic. It's easier to pretend that it's never going to happen."

"Well, my advice would be to just talk about it. Rip off the Band-Aid... see where his head's at, you know?"

"Yeah, you're right. We're going hiking today, so maybe I'll bring it up then. It depends on his mood, though. He won't open up with me and tell me what he's thinking unless he's in the right mood. But we'll see. I've gotta run; I'll talk to you soon, okay?"

"Okay, bye! Have fun! Text me a picture of you guys on your hike!"

I hang up the phone, send my last email of the morning, and head to my bedroom. I'm supposed to meet John in twenty minutes for our hike. I dig through the dresser and pull out a matching workout set. I pull on the black yoga pants and black sports bra, and wrap a black and white flannel button up around my waist just in case, although I don't think I'll need it. As I pull my tennis shoes on, I hear a knock at the door and the creak of the front door opening.

"Mia?"

"Come on in! I'll be right there!"

I tie up my laces, and then stop in the bathroom to pull my hair up into a ponytail and apply some sunscreen. Walking back down the hallway, I see John leaning against the back of the couch, waiting patiently. My heart skips a beat. He's wearing a pair of gray basketball shorts and a black T-shirt. I walk up to him and lean into his chest. His strong arms encircle me, and if this isn't the best feeling in the whole wide world, I don't know what is.

I squeeze him tighter, and then remove myself from his arms, walking to the front door. "Are you ready to hike? I can't believe you have all these amazing trails here, and you hardly ever go!"

"I'm not a big hiker, but I'll suck it up and go for you," he says with a smile. "You came fishing with me, so it's only fair."

"That's right! I went fishing AND got sea sick for you," I say, leaning over to give him a quick kiss as we close the cottage door. "And I'd do it all over again every single day because I saw how happy it made you."

"You're amazing, you know that?" He grabs my hand as we make our way to his car.

"I know," I reply with a smirk.

We drive about fifteen minutes to get to Manoa Falls Trail. It's supposed to be a relatively easy trail, which is why I chose it. It's only 1.6 miles, so it shouldn't take us too long. If it's not too miserable for him, maybe I'll be able to convince him to go on a longer hike with me another time. We park and climb out of the car, spray some mosquito repellant on ourselves, and make our way to the entrance. We set off on the trail, and I'm caught off guard by how stunning it already is. It feels like I just walked into a rainforest. I can smell the eucalyptus trees, and it's misting rain, which is crazy because it was bright and sunny on the drive over. The light rain makes the trail a little muddy, so we hold hands to keep each other steady.

We continue on, passing breathtaking banyan trees, marveling at the way their many roots grow intertwined with each other. I take a selfie of us standing in front of one to send to Paige. After a little while, we come to a detour that takes us through a bamboo grove. We walk mostly in silence, taking in the stunning beauty. Eventually, we reach the 100-foot-high waterfall. Even though the flow isn't too hard, given the lack of rain recently, it is still absolutely stunning. We walk up to the wooden fence surrounding the water below the waterfall.

"It's beautiful, isn't it?" I ask John, who nods in agreement. "Should we rest here for a few minutes before finishing the trail?"

"Sure."

We both lean against the fence, taking it all in. I figure now is as good a time as any to bring up what we should do once I go home. I hesitate, not sure if I can manage to keep up a good face if he doesn't want to keep in touch.

Band-Aid, Mia. Rip the Band-Aid off.

"So… "I start, turning toward him. "Do you think we should maybe… talk about us? I'm supposed to leave in a couple of weeks, and I guess I just want to see where your head is at."

John angles his body so his hip is leaning against the fence, facing me. His eyes meet mine, and he nods. "Yeah, that's probably a good idea."

"I mean, I don't want to put pressure on this or anything... and if you don't want to keep talking to me after I leave, I totally under—"

"Would you stay?" he interrupts. My eyes grow wide as I take in what he just said. "What do you mean *stay?*"

"I mean, I know this is relatively new, and I still think you deserve someone a hell of a lot better than me, and I know it's not really fair of me to ask you to stay... but would you? Stay?

With me, obviously," he asks with a hint of nervousness in his voice.

I'm surprised at how much I want to say absolutely and jump in his arms. Being on this hike with John makes me long for a life full of adventures with him. My heart is desperately screaming at me to say yes. It's my brain that's making me pause before agreeing to uproot my entire life. Would it be absolutely insane? Yes, yes, it would. I hadn't even allowed my brain to consider staying as an option.

"You want me to move in with you?"

"Yes... if you wanted to."

I let out a small laugh that sounds slightly crazed even to my ears. "I mean, how would that work? I would probably have to leave my job back home and find a new job here, and I'd be leaving my friends and family. I don't know... it's a lot, John. I guess I need to think about it?" He nods in understanding. As frazzled as I am, I can't help the smile forming on my face. "I'm flattered that you asked, though. I like you a lot, John. I've never felt this with anyone else—you know that, right?"

He grabs my hand and moves to stand in front of me. I wrap my other arm around his neck as he gives me a sweet smile.

"Yes, I know that. I've never felt like this with anyone else either. I'd be stupid to let you go without at least trying to get you to stay." He leans down to kiss my lips, and I can't help but think of how amazing it would be to get to kiss him every day.

We spend a few minutes kissing, listening to the waterfall trickle down and drip into the pool of water next to us. Then we make our way down the rest of the trail to finish our hiking adventure for the day. When we reach the car, we grab some water bottles from the cooler that John put in his trunk. John tosses me a towel and grabs one for himself, and we attempt to clean some of the mud off of our shoes before we get back in the car.

"Thank you for coming with me today, John. I had a really great time. It wasn't so bad, was it?"

"You're welcome," he says with a smile. "I'm starting to think you could talk me into doing just about anything with you."

I grin back at him, climbing in the car. On the drive back, I can't help but think that I'm the same way with him. I'm not exactly sure what a life with John would look like, but I do know without a doubt that I don't like the idea of a life *without* him. And that alone scares me to death.

22

MIA

The next morning, after my run on the beach, I take my laptop into town so I can work for a few hours at Julie's. I order my usual—an Americano with one pump of vanilla—and sit down while Julie gets it ready. I open my laptop and log in to my work email. Hazel must be in school today, because her usual spot is empty. The coffee shop has a whole different energy without her here, and I find myself missing her constant chatter.

"Here you go, honey!" Julie calls out to me. I go up to the counter and grab my drink. "Thanks, Julie! You're the best." The coffee shop's not too busy, so she leans on the counter toward me.

"What have you been up to? When do you leave again?"

I fill her in on our recent adventures, leaving out the part about possibly staying in Hawaii permanently. No need to share that with people until I make up my mind.

"Sounds like you've been having a blast! I'll let ya get to

work over there. Let me know if you need anything else!" She retreats back to the cash register to help the customer who just walked in.

"Sounds good. Thanks, Julie!" I sit back down and pull up the article I need to edit today. This one is a review of a new restaurant that just opened in downtown Minneapolis. As I read through the piece, I think about everything I would miss about home if I moved here. As much as I dislike the cold winters, it's not all bad. And you pretty much can't beat Minnesota in the summer. The perfect weather, the 10,000 lakes, the cabins, the boating, the restaurants... I could go on and on. Not to mention how much I would miss my family and friends. I'd also have to go through the hassle of finding a new job—my boss has been great about letting me work remotely for a while, but I know she wouldn't be okay with making that a permanent thing.

Is John worth it? *Yes. He is.*

But at the same time, how am I supposed to just change my entire life for someone who isn't giving me all of himself? Not that I feel like I need him to tell me everything he experienced in Iraq—I don't need that at all. I would listen to anything he wanted to tell me about his time in the military, but I wouldn't blame him if he didn't want to put that on me. I just hate the fact that he is struggling so much that he literally can't bring himself to talk about it to *anyone*.

I know how important communication is in a relationship, so would we be doomed if we started off this way? Ugh, I don't know. I guess I have some more thinking to do.

I work at the coffee shop for a couple more hours, then walk over to the Farmers Market to pick up some food. I browse leisurely, taking my time, daydreaming about calling this place home. Does it feel right? Could I picture a life here? As much as I would miss home, living here happily wouldn't be that far out of reach. Not just because it's literally paradise. I wouldn't move away from my family and Paige just for paradise. However, I would move away from them for the kind of love I can see having with John. On the Uber ride back to the cottage, I send him a text.

Mia: Will you go on a date with me tonight?

John: Of course. Where can I take you?

Mia: I'd love to go to that seafood place where you got the poke bowls from? Can we go there?

John: You betcha.

I let out a laugh.

Mia: Have you been brushing up on your Minnesotan lingo? I'm so proud.

John: Doing my best! Pick you up at 5?

Mia: Can't wait!

When I get back to the cottage, I hop in the shower and take my time getting ready for our date. I choose a mustard yellow sundress that has a deep V-neck and hits a few inches above my knee. While I wait for the curling iron to warm up, I go into the closet and pull out some tan, strappy sandals and gold hoop earrings.

After curling my hair, I put my phone in my purse, grab the cottage keys, and head out the door. I am halfway to the house when John opens the sliding door and steps outside. He is looking extra handsome tonight, wearing khaki shorts and a navy blue polo shirt—Hawaii's version of business casual. His brown eyes light up when he sees me, and then they give me a leisurely scan from my head down to my feet and back up again. When his eyes meet mine, it's obvious he appreciates my efforts. The heat in his eyes sends a shiver down my spine.

"I was just coming to get you," he says, pulling me to him in a hug. "I know," I reply, wrapping my arms around him. "I was ready early so I figured I'd come to you." He doesn't let me go, just holds me tighter, burying his face in my hair, and eventually I laugh and try to wiggle away from him. "Come on, let's go! I'm getting hungry!"

"Fine," he says with a sigh, letting me go and settling for holding my hand. When we reach the car, he opens the passenger door for me. "What a gentleman... thank you."

I slide into the seat and watch him walk around the front of the car to the driver's side. He lowers himself into the seat, while simultaneously reaching for my hand, like it was a terrible inconvenience to have parted with it. I don't mind one bit. I smile at him, and we drive into town.

We make it to the restaurant and head inside. The hostess leads us to a small booth in the far back corner of the restaurant. She hands us some menus as we slide into the booth, meeting in the middle, the sides of our bodies pressed firmly together. It is nice and cozy. Our waitress comes by and we put in our drink orders: wine for me, beer for John. When she leaves the table, I ask John his opinion of a few things on the menu.

Not wanting to stray from a good thing once I find it, I decide to stick with the Ahi tuna poke bowl. John decides on a build-your-own bowl with brown rice, marinated sesame salmon, edamame, scallions, and avocado in a samurai sauce. Our waitress arrives to bring us our drinks, we give her our food order, and she leaves to go ring it in.

I take a sip of my wine, and peer over at John. I am amazed at the difference between this John and the John that went out to dinner with me that first night at The Toasted Crab. He seems so much more at ease right now—less stiff, less anxious.

"Can I ask you a question?" I ask him.

He turns his head so his attention is all on me. "Sure."

"Is it easier for you to go to a restaurant now than it was before? I know you don't like being in a crowded place, around a lot of people."

"It is easier. I feel like I can actually take a deep breath right now, and I only feel a little tense, when it used to all be so overwhelming." I feel a rush of pride that he's willing to tell me that. I love it when he opens up and gives me a peek at what he's feeling.

His mouth curves up into a slanted smile. "I owe that to you, you know. You've helped me more than you could imagine." His words make me blush.

"Oh, I don't know about that. I didn't really do anything."

"You did." He kisses my cheek, and a flood of warmth spreads through my body.

Gosh, I think I love this man.

That realization surprises me, but only partially. I think a part of me has been in love with him since the moment I laid eyes on him. Almost like my soul knew we were meant for each other before my mind did. It just took longer for the rest of me to figure it out. But yes, now that I think about it—I am absolutely head over heels, overwhelmingly in love with John.

Now, am I going to profess my newly realized love? Heck no. I'm going to sit back and wait for him to say it first... it's safer that way. I don't usually put my heart on the line first, and I definitely won't this time. Not when some parts of John are still such a mystery to me. I think he loves me, too, but can I really be certain?

Our food arrives, and we enjoy our meal. I had talked to my mom this morning, so we chat about what they were up to back at home. "Would you ever go to Minnesota? I know you said you've never really been anywhere in the Midwest... but do you have any desire to?" I ask.

"Sure, I'd go. I've always wanted to try snowboarding." He looks at me. "I'd go just about anywhere with you." He smiles at me, taking another bite of food. Yup, I like that answer.

Not that I want John to move to Minnesota with me. I'm not sure if he's in the right headspace to make a major move like that. But, I definitely like that he offered to go.

We finish our meal, and John pays the tab. "Do you want to go say hi to Matt? He's working tonight, right?" I ask.

John nods in confirmation. "Sure, I'd be up for that. Let's go." It's just a few blocks until we get to The Toasted Crab. We walk in and find two open seats at the bar. I hop onto one, while John sits on the stool to my right. Matt is busy pouring drinks on the other end of the bar, but he glances over and grins at us. "Heyyyy, what's happening? You two look nice and cozy." He directs his gaze to me. "Is John taking good care of you? Cause if you're getting lonely over there in that cottage all by yourself, I'd happily volunteer myself—"

"All right, all right," John huffs. "I'll have a Gold Cliff. Mia?"

"Can I have one of those hibiscus mai tais again, please?" I'm more of a wine girl, but I figure I should take advantage of all the yummy tropical drinks here while I can.

"You got it." Matt winks and backs away.

"Does he wink at all of his customers?" I ask John, who laughs out loud.

"Just the pretty ones," he replies dryly.

I set my phone on the counter, and John does the same. Matt sets our drinks on coasters and leans over the bar. "What's new? You been doing any more fishing?"

John shakes his head. "Nah, no more fishing."

"I'd like to go again, though! See if I can get through a whole trip without puking," I say, making John and Matt laugh. We chit-chat for a few minutes, then Matt backs away to tend to his customers.

John takes a sip of his beer, when I notice his phone light up. *Text message from Adam Hanson,* it says.

"Hey, you have a message from Adam." I say casually, taking a sip of my mai tai. I immediately regret opening my mouth, because John visibly tenses. He grabs the phone and clears the message without opening it.

"Who's Adam?"

"Mia... drop it." He puts his phone in his pocket, then slides off the stool. "I need some air," he says, already walking toward the door.

Um, okay...

I stare after him for a minute, my mouth open in confusion. "He all right?" Matt asks behind me. I turn to face him and shrug.

"I have no idea... he got a text message and just completely shut down and went outside."

Matt looks towards the door, brows furrowed in worry. Then he gives me a sympathetic smile, his face softening. "He's been through a lot, you know? He won't open up to me about anything, but I know he must have gone through hell. He came home a very different man than the one who left."

"I know. Sometimes I don't know how to respond. I don't know if I'm doing the right thing, you know?"

He gives me a reassuring smile. "I will say this... whatever you've been doing, it's working. You're good for him, Mia. I gotta get back to work, but let me know if you need anything." I give him a weak smile and sip my drink.

After twenty minutes or so, I start to wonder if I should go look for John. I'm just about to hop off my stool when I feel his hand on my back. "I'm sorry," he says, but gives me nothing more. We sip the rest of our drinks in silence, and not a word is spoken the whole way home.

23

MIA

I wake up with John behind me, his arm draped around me. I can feel his breath softly exhaling on the back of my neck. I roll over very gently so I'm facing him and tuck myself under his head, getting as close as I possibly can. My arms are curled in front of me, resting on the brick wall that is his stomach. I feel his arm tighten around my back.

"I'm sorry about last night," he whispers, his jaw resting on the top of my head.

"It's okay," I whisper.

He shakes his head. "No, it's not."

I'm not sure what to say next, so I don't say anything for a while.

"Let's go to the beach today," I suggest, knowing that the ocean always seems to help him. Maybe surfing can be my backup therapy today... God knows I'm running out of ideas on how to get through to him.

"That sounds good."

I let him hold me, soaking him up, trying to forget about last night. I wish we could stay in this bed together forever, with his arm around me, where I feel so connected to him. He squeezes me tighter, kisses the top of my head, and then rolls the other way to climb out of bed. I watch him go, until he's all the way out of sight, then throw back the covers. I pull on my olive green swimsuit and throw my black cover-up over it. After brushing my teeth and pulling my hair up into a bun, I walk into the kitchen, where John's laid a bowl of cereal and a plate of papaya out for me.

"You know the way to my heart," I say with a smile. He's leaning against the counter, sipping coffee. He gives me a gentle smile and watches me while I eat my breakfast. After the kitchen is cleaned up, we grab some towels and head over to the house so John can throw on some swim trunks.

"Do you want to grab your surfboard?" I ask as we walk through the garage to the driveway.

"Nah, I don't feel like surfing today."

"Oh, okay." He takes my hand, and we walk in silence past Rose's house to the beach access trail. Once we make it onto the beach, we find a spot to sit and lay out our towels. Before I sit, I have a better idea.

"I think I'm gonna go for a swim—wanna come?" I ask him, pulling my cover-up over my head.

"Sure," John replies.

"Race you!" I call out as I start jogging. John's face breaks out into a grin as he starts charging for me. Next thing I know, we're sprinting towards the water like two kids without a care in the world.

My feet splash into the turquoise water two seconds behind John's. Laughing loudly, I do a small victory dance before I wade into the water. Sighing, I spread my arms out wide and tilt my head back to feel the sun. I feel a strong, muscular arm wrap around my middle, and I squeal as John pulls me deeper into the water.

His arm still firmly around me, he backs up until the ocean is up to my shoulders. He pulls me closer, and I wrap my legs around his waist, winding my arms around his shoulders. His hands slide to my butt and stay planted there as he carries me around in the water. His hands radiate heat, the contact sending waves of warmth rushing through me. My body always responds to his touch, and I wonder if that would ever go away.

"This is nice... I could stay like this forever," I murmur into his ear. He pulls back slightly to look me in the eyes.

"You can."

"You'd carry me around everywhere?" I ask with a smile.

He responds by giving me one of the warm smiles I love so much. "I'd carry you anywhere you want to go." His expression shifts, and he transforms into serious John. "Have you thought any more about moving here?"

"I've been thinking about it a lot, actually. I really want to, John. I can't imagine leaving you now, but I'm scared."

He nods. "It's a big decision."

"I just need more time to think about it, okay?"

"Take all the time you need. I only want you to stay if it's what you really want to do."

I give him a soft smile in response, feeling a small wave crash into our shoulders. I wonder if things would be different if he knew the key to me staying is giving me more of what's inside him. If he did, I would stay in a heartbeat.

We swim around—or rather, John carries me around—for a while until he reluctantly releases me so we can walk back to our towels.

"Do you want to walk down the beach to that little tiki hut and grab some burritos for lunch?" I ask, drying my arms with the towel.

"Sure," he replies, reaching for his sunglasses. We walk

along the beach, stopping at the tiki hut and eating our burritos on the walk back. We spend another two hours lying on the beach, soaking up the sun. Eventually, we pack up our towels and head back to the house.

"What do you want to do for dinner?" I ask on the walk back.

"I have chicken in the fridge; why don't we grill out by the pool and then bring it back to the cottage to eat? I don't know about you, but I've had enough sun for the day."

"That sounds wonderful! I just need a quick shower first." When we arrive at the cottage, I go straight to the laundry room and throw our towels in the washing machine, start it up, and then turn toward the bathroom. I round the corner and find John propped up on the wall, waiting.

He gives me a devilish grin. "What a coincidence. I happen to need a shower, too." His arms come around me, and he dance-walks me backward toward the bathroom.

My mouth curls up into a flirtatious smile. "Is that so?"

"Yup." He picks me up and carries me towards the shower, peppering kisses on my neck as one hand reaches to turn the shower on. He gently sets me on my feet so he can peel my swimsuit off, unfastening the straps in the back first and letting the top fall to the ground. He slips his hands down to my hips and inside my swimsuit bottoms, sliding them slowly down until I kick them aside. I return the favor by untying and pulling down his swim trunks. He picks me back up and climbs into the shower, where he so graciously helps me get clean.

"That was so good," I say as I walk an empty plate over to the sink. John comes up behind me, sets the salad bowl in the sink, then places a hand on my low back, kissing my cheek.

"It was. Thanks for making the salad."

"Of course. It was the least I could do." John clears the rest of the table while I load the dishes in the dishwasher. Grabbing another plate to rinse, I hear my phone ring on the counter. "Hey, do you mind seeing who that is? My hands are all wet." It's silent for a few moments, except for the sound of my phone ringing.

"John?"

"Sean," John says in a cold, flat voice.

"What?" I turn around, and John must miss the confusion on my face because he asks, "Why is Sean calling your phone?"

"Uh, I have no idea. I haven't spoken to him since I left home, so I'm not sure why he would be calling."

The phone stops ringing as it sends Sean to voicemail.

"Are you gonna call him back?" John asks sharply. His tone is intense, and demanding. My stomach starts to sink, not fully understanding his reaction.

"Um… I'm not sure... I mean, probably? I guess to see what he wants?"

"Are you serious? Why would you talk to him?" he asks, growing angrier by the second. His face is turning red, and his eyes are burning into mine.

Wait… what?

Why is he mad at me? I'm stunned at his reaction, and I feel prickles of anger starting to build in my chest.

"Hold on—you can't seriously be upset with me right now because Sean called my phone."

"I'm not. I'm irritated that you would want to call him back and talk to him." He huffs and crosses his arms over his chest.

I blink a few times, staring at him, wondering for a brief second if I should give him space to cool off, but anger takes over, and I shake my head.

"I'm sorry, but you don't get to be mad at me right now." My voice gets louder as disbelief and anger rise within me. "That's not fair at all. I can't talk to my ex—who I have known most of my life—yet you won't even tell me who a simple person is that texted *you?*" I dry my hands on the towel and march into the living room, unable to stop fuming at his hypocrisy. Spinning around, I point my finger at him.

"Who the hell is Adam, John? Huh? You won't tell me who he even is to you, yet you can be mad that someone from my life —who you know all about, by the way—calls my phone? Are you serious right now?"

John continues to glare at me, clenching his jaw. I shake my head. "I think I've been more than patient with you, John. Is it too much to ask that you do the same for me?" I ask, my voice coming back down to normal. He gives me nothing, just his eyes piercing into mine.

"That's it? You're not gonna say anything?" I let out a sigh and look at the floor. I'm so frustrated I can't stand to even look at him right now.

"Maybe you should go," I say quietly. I refuse to look up, but out of the corner of my eye I can see John move quickly toward the door and shut it gently behind him. The sound of the door clicking shut causes a rush of dread to flow through me. I collapse onto the couch and let the tears stream down my face. How did this night end up this way? What the hell is his problem, coming at me like that? Unbelievable.

I sit for a few minutes to let my anger cool down, taking a couple of deep breaths. When I finally feel calmer, I glance out the window over at the main house. The lights are off, which means he probably went right to his bedroom. I start to feel disgusted with myself, because all I can think about is how I know John hates to sleep alone.

Really, Mia? Don't cave. Hold your ground.

I ignore myself, and against my better judgment, I change into my pajamas and walk out the cottage door. The entire walk over, I question what the hell I'm doing. Am I sacrificing my own feelings for the sake of his? To make him feel more comfortable? The simple answer would be yes, but I can't bring myself to turn around.

When I reach the sliding pool door, I find it unlocked. Knowing John usually locks it at night, I take that as an invitation. An olive branch. I open the door and slip inside, walking quietly down the hall, not wanting to wake him. I don't want to talk to him right now, I just want to crawl into bed and fall asleep—which is exactly what I do.

24

JOHN

Sitting on my couch, I bring the coffee mug to my mouth and sip on the black coffee. I crept out here to the living room early so I wouldn't wake Mia. I felt her slip into bed last night, but I figured we both needed some space, so I didn't say anything.

Ugh, last night. What a fucking disaster. My chest aches, and I feel sick to my stomach. I wish I was better at communicating. I just can't seem to form the right words to explain how I'm feeling. I hadn't meant for it to escalate as much as it did; I was just caught off guard and maybe a little scared. Did she talk to him often? Was Sean calling her a regular thing? I already have plenty of insecurities about being good enough for Mia—there's no doubt in my mind that she deserves someone who can give her all of himself—so I guess I kind of shut down when I saw his name.

The sound of light footsteps brings me out of my thoughts, and I look up to see Mia, in her black polka-dotted pajama shirt and shorts, leaning against the door frame. I take her in to see if I can gauge what kind of mood she's in or what she's thinking, but her face gives nothing away. She walks over slowly and sits on the coffee table, facing me, her knees in between mine.

"We need to talk about this," she says firmly. I nod slowly, not sure that I'm ready to hear what she has to say or that I'll even be able to put words together to tell her what I was thinking.

"I'll start," Mia says, bringing her eyes to meet mine and locking them in place. "This isn't fair to me, John, and you know it. This isn't about Sean—forget about him. We could have had a calm, adult conversation last night, and instead, you completely blew it out of proportion. You shut down and shut me out, just like you do all the time, and that's a huge problem." She continues in a calm, even way that makes me wonder if she's rehearsed this. "How am I supposed to completely uproot my entire life for someone who won't let me in? Explain that, will you? Because I can't make it make sense." Her words hit me like a punch to the stomach, confirming my insecurities.

You're right. It isn't fair.

"Are we really supposed to just live a life where we sweep everything under the rug and not address it? When you shut down, am I supposed to just ride it out and wait for you to come back to me? Is that really how you expect this to go? I don't want to have to walk on eggshells all the time, never knowing how you're going to react or what you're thinking."

You're right. You deserve so much better.

My eyes focus on hers, but I can't think of the right words to say. My mind is whirling like a hurricane. Would she be better off without me? Absolutely. I can't give her everything she needs, and that shatters me in every possible way. Her eyebrows rise up, and she stares back at me, expectantly.

"Are you really not gonna say anything?" She gently pushes my shoulders back and sits on my lap, straddling me on the couch. Both of her hands come to the sides of my face, and she tilts my head up to meet hers. I bring my hands to rest on her hips, frantically clinging to this small connection that seems to be all I can give her.

"John... let me in," she begs, the pain in her voice obvious, and desperation in her eyes. "Please... let me in."

I feel like a concrete statue, frozen, unable to say anything.

She puts her forehead on mine and shakes her head. "John... I love you."

My eyes fly up to meet hers, startled by her admission. "I love you, John," she repeats. "Do you love me?" I see tears forming in her eyes, and I can't help the ones that start forming in mine.

Do I love you? Yes. Am I good enough for you? Absolutely not.

My silence is enough for her to bring her face away from mine and sit back on my legs, putting more space between us. Tears are now free-flowing down her cheeks, and that only adds to the heartache and tightness in my chest. She pushes her lips together and nods slowly.

"Okay... do you even like me, John? Or do you just want me around 'cause I make you feel less shitty?" I wince at her words. She backs off my lap, and it takes a massive amount of restraint not to reach out and grab her. But I know what's best for her... and it's not me.

"I can't do this anymore, John," she whispers, her voice breaking, and she walks to the sliding door.

Wait... I'm sorry... I do love you... please don't go.

The door clicks shut, and I officially break down. Uncontrollable sobs break from my chest, and I cover my face with my hands. I've spent the last several months suppressing every terrible feeling I have, but now I can't seem to lock it down. Despair, anguish, and regret sweep through me, over and over again, and I feel absolutely broken. I lean over on the couch to lay down, and I just let myself feel. Feel it all. Let it fully break me, so maybe I'll have a fighting chance at putting it all back together the right way.

I'm not sure how much time passes, but eventually, I peel myself off the couch and go to my room and turn the light off. I don't want to leave the house, I don't want to go outside, I don't even want to see the sun through the window. I want to stay in this dark room with my dark emotions until I figure out what the hell I need to do to put my life back together. I'm tired of living like this and pushing everyone I love away.

Eventually, I fall asleep, utterly exhausted from my emotional breakdown. When I wake up, I glance at my clock and realize I slept for most of the day. It's already 7:30 p.m. I grab my phone, hoping to find a missed call or message from Mia. All I see is a missed call from Quinn. I climb out of bed and make my way to the kitchen for something to drink. Grabbing a beer from the fridge, I look out the window to the cottage. It's dark outside now, but the lights inside the cottage are on.

Mia's in there.

A part of me is longing to go over there and see her, but a bigger part of me—the broken part—knows that she was right. It's not fair of me to ask her to commit to me when I'm unable to fully commit to her. I turn the kitchen light back off, and walk back down the dark hallway to my dark room. I climb under the covers and fall back to sleep, this time into a familiar dream.

Iraq

"I'm sorry," Sergeant Cooper says, placing a hand on my back. "This is an unimaginable loss for all of us. Take some time and regroup. I need to make some phone calls so we can notify next of kin." He leaves me on my cot, tears streaming down my face, trying to absorb everything that just happened.

Next of kin. Fuck.

Connor has a fiancée back home in Connecticut, as well as his parents and other family members. The wedding date is set for next summer. I had already booked a flight so I could go. Luis has a wife, a three-year-old, and a baby on the way back in Virginia. It absolutely crushes me that they'll be getting that knock on the door with the uniformed men who bring unbearable news.

I blow out a breath, thinking of my other two brothers who lost their lives today. Their families will be completely devastated as well. It's just not fair; why them? Obviously, when you join the military, and especially when you're deployed, your own death, as well as the death of your brothers, is always a possibility, but that doesn't make it any less devastating.

Four soldiers dead. And why? I mean, yes, we were under enemy fire, so any one of us could have been taken out—luckily, Langston wasn't seriously injured when he was shot—but to lose four men from a mistake made by our own people? Absolutely crushing. What the hell was Adam thinking?

As if summoned by my own thoughts, Adam slowly stumbles in the tent. He looks dazed, utterly confused, and heartbroken. As he should. He walks to the cot next to me, sits down, and turns his head to face me. That's when I see the true anguish on his face.

"John…"

I cut him off. "Don't," I sigh. "Listen… I know it was a mistake. I'm just not ready to talk about this yet, okay?" Before he can say another word, I get up and walk out of the tent to find Sergeant Cooper. My tour is set to come to an end in two weeks, and I need to tell him I will not be extending this time. I'm done.

. . .

I awake with a start, breathing heavily and sweating. I bring my hands to my face, which feels wet. I must have been crying. Usually, my night terrors give me more of a physical response, with my heart racing, shaky hands, etc. But this time, it seemed to be more of an emotional release. My pillow is soaking wet from my tears. I'm guessing it was probably tied to the emotions from yesterday with Mia. I take a few deep breaths and shake my head. Every inch of my body feels completely exhausted and sore. I walk out to the kitchen to see that it's 8:30 a.m. and another bright and sunny day. I glance over at the cottage and stop in my tracks when I see Mia coming down the stairs, carrying her luggage.

My heart breaks again into a million pieces when the realization hits me that she must be leaving. Going home. To Minnesota. An Uber pulls into the driveway and stops by the cottage.

Do I go out there? Do I say something? What would I say?

No. I'm not any more of a whole man than I was yesterday, maybe even less so now. She doesn't need me to confuse her or add to her heartbreak. I've caused enough pain. So instead, I watch as she throws her suitcases into the trunk and climbs into the passenger seat. Then the car backs up and slowly drives away with the most significant person in my life... who never once looks back.

25

MIA

I keep my eyes focused on my hands in my lap the entire ride to the airport. I don't want to look out the window. I don't want to see Hawaii. The beautiful scenery, the beach, the coffee shop, the bar, all the places that were starting to feel like mine... the places that were almost my home... I can't bear to see. I didn't even give the main house or the cottage a second look when I left because it would have reduced me to a puddle on the ground. It took every last bit of strength in me to just get myself and my stuff in the car.

Technically, I still had several days left before I was supposed to fly home. But how could I stay? How could I stay after I poured my heart out and begged John to love me, and he wouldn't. He couldn't. He didn't offer a single word to me. I know he has a hard time expressing himself and communicating, and I think I've been more than patient and understanding with that. But I can't do it anymore. I'm not going to leave my old life behind for a new life that doesn't have a strong foundation. As much as it kills me, I know I'm making the right choice.

After I left John yesterday, I spent the day in the cottage, packing, booking an earlier flight, and talking to my mom and Paige. I filled them in on everything, and they were patient listeners, as always. I can't wait to get home and hug them. And my dad, who is picking me up from the airport. I couldn't help but sneak a few glances at the main house while I was packing, but the house was completely dark. I had to talk myself out of worrying about him, reminding myself that I was done putting his needs before mine. This was the last straw.

After about twenty minutes of successfully avoiding looking outside, the car finally arrives at the airport and comes to a stop. "Thank you," I murmur to the driver, and then get out to grab my luggage. I wheel a cart over and place everything on top, then start pushing it into the airport. I make it all the way through baggage claim, security, and find my gate. While waiting for boarding to start, I pass the time by thinking of my trip to Hawaii as a whole. I had initially come needing a change of scenery, a fresh outlook on life after Sean. While I was here, I happened to fall in love with a man who was battling demons much bigger than anything I've ever experienced. My mom had warned me about going home with a broken heart, and she was right.

I pull out my phone and call Paige, desperate to hear her voice. She answers on the second ring.

"Mia?" She sounds worried.

"Yeah, hi. I just needed to talk to somebody. I made it to the airport." I can barely muster a whisper.

"Oh, Mia… I'm so sorry you're going through this. I wish there was something I could do."

"I'll be okay… I think."

"You know what? I'm gonna pick up some essentials—ice cream, wine, chocolate—and I'll meet you at your place when you get home, okay? We'll get through this together, like we always do." I smile, comforted by her offer.

"I appreciate it, Paige, but don't bother. I'm probably just gonna crash when I get home. Jet lag is gonna be ugly. Can you come over tomorrow, though?"

"Of course."

"Oh, they're just starting to board, so I'll talk to you later. Thanks, Paige... I've really missed you."

"I can't wait to see you. Have a good flight, and I'll see you soon."

My row is finally called, and I board the plane. I get settled in my seat, close the window shade, and pull my eye mask over my eyes, hoping it will help to cover the tears that will surely come. I don't even bother to notice if anyone is sitting next to me. I'm not in the mood to talk to anyone right now.

Eventually, the plane takes off, and I spend the next nine hours nursing my broken heart, desperately missing the only person who could make it whole again.

"There's my peanut!" Dad smiles as he pulls me in for a hug. I'm too tired to roll my eyes at his nickname for me, so I just smile and hug him back.

"Hi, Dad." He grabs my luggage cart and pushes it towards the exit.

"Welcome home, you ready to go?" he asks as he throws his arm around my shoulder. I nod, and we make our way out the door to his car that is waiting for us outside. The cold air blasts my face, and I'm glad to see that it's warmed up to a balmy 32 degrees.

Once we're in the car, he pulls away from the airport en route to Maple Grove, where my apartment is.

"So, did you have nice weather on your trip? I saw it was in the 80s pretty much every day you were there." I smile, appreciating the fact that he's avoiding bringing up John. "The weather was great," I reply. We chat the whole ride home, mostly about some new restaurants he and mom went to while I was away. I try to put all of my focus on him and what he's saying, but my mind keeps drifting to John and how much I miss him. At one point, I pull down the visor and peek at myself in the mirror. I'm not surprised to see that my eyes are all puffy from crying on the plane.

He pulls into my apartment parking lot and parks. My shoes crunch on snow as I step out of the car. Dad helps me carry my luggage up to my apartment on the second floor. Once inside, I thank my dad and shoo him out the door, telling him I'm exhausted and need a nap. I shut the door, turn around, and look around my apartment. It's a cute one-bedroom unit with gray walls and white trim. The kitchen is to the left when you walk in, connected to a small living room, and then the hallway to the bathroom and bedroom are on the right.

I love my apartment, and usually look forward to coming home, but it feels different this time. It's like the connection I once felt here is gone. I let out a deep breath. I was ready to give all this up to be with John. Even though I hadn't made up my mind yet about staying in Hawaii, a part of me had started to let this apartment go. This doesn't feel like home to me now, either. No place feels like home except John. He is my home. Except my home doesn't want me, and I need to come to terms with that.

Maybe I should have agreed to let Paige meet me here. Being by myself in this apartment feels so depressing now. I take a deep breath and bend down to pick up one of my suitcases, when I hear a knock on my door. Surprised, I open the door to find Paige holding a grocery bag.

All of a sudden, the tears are uncontrollable. I'm so thankful she didn't listen to me; I really need my best friend right now. She gives me a sympathetic smile, sets the bag down, and throws her arms around me in a hug. I can't hold back at all anymore, and she lets me hang onto her, my tears soaking her shoulder, until I'm too exhausted to stand anymore.

She shoos me over to the couch while she starts scooping ice cream into bowls. When she walks over to me, I can't help but laugh at the huge bowl she filled for me. It's nearly overflowing with chocolate ice cream, my favorite. She pulls out a bottle of red wine and pours a couple glasses for us, setting the bottle on the coffee table in front of us.

"You know what?" she says, her eyes lighting up. "I have an even better idea." She grabs the wine and pours some directly into my bowl of ice cream. "Desperate times call for desperate measures." I can't help but laugh through my tears.

"What would I do without you, Paige?"

"Well, you'd probably be wallowing and feeling sorry for yourself. Which you can totally still do, by the way. But at least you won't be alone." She gives me a smile. "How are you feeling?"

I let out a deep breath. "I'm heartbroken, Paige. I love him, I really do. I keep wondering if I made the right choice by coming home. He clearly needs help. Maybe I should have stayed to make sure he'll be okay."

"I get it, but honey, there's only so much you can do for another person. You can't make him get help if he doesn't want it for himself."

"I know… that's what I keep reminding myself." I take a bite of my ice cream-slash-wine and discover that it's actually not bad.

"Do you want to watch a movie?"

"Not really…. I just want to eat my boozy ice cream and go to sleep. Is that all right?"

"Of course."

We finish our ice cream in silence. One of the things I love about my friendship with Paige is that while we both love to talk, we don't need to fill the silence with words. Right now, I appreciate her silent support more than she knows. When I bring our bowls to the kitchen, she doesn't even ask if I'd like her to stay. She just follows me to my room, where we get ready for bed. After I brush my teeth, I climb into bed, with Paige right next to me, holding my hand, and I allow the endless tears to continue.

Two weeks later

"There you are!" Paige calls as she rushes to the table and gives me a quick hug. We're meeting during our lunch breaks at one of our favorite little cafes. She pulls her chair out and sits down. "How's work going today?" she asks.

"It's going okay. You know, the usual. Nothing too crazy. How about you?" Paige is a second-grade teacher at an elementary school in Plymouth. She doesn't have a long lunch break, so we're meeting at the cafe that's right down the street from her school. "Oh, it's good! Second-graders are something else, man. If I have to hear one more story about aliens invading earth and sucking up cows into their spaceships…" She shakes her head.

I laugh. Paige always has the best stories about the things her students say. I try not to think of Hazel every time she brings up her students, but it's been hard not to. Dang, I miss that girl. I didn't even have a chance to say goodbye before I left.

She gives me a sympathetic smile. "How've you been doing?

Honestly? Has it gotten any easier being home? Or do you still miss him?" Of course, I miss him. I miss him with every fiber of my being. Every little thing reminds me of him. I can't sleep because I know he's not sleeping well either, without me, and every single day I have to talk myself out of just jumping on a plane and flying back to him.

"Yeah, I miss him a lot." There isn't much else to say that hasn't already been said. Paige has spent nearly every day with me since I've been back, bringing me food or dragging me out to go to the mall or one of our favorite restaurants. We've also had our fair share of wine and ice cream in the last two weeks. I don't know what I would do without her; she truly is the best.

She nods in understanding. "That sucks. And still no word from him?" I shake my head. "Nope." Our food arrives, and we start eating our salads.

"Guess who did call me last night, though," I say.

Her brow lifts in surprise. "Sean?"

"Yup. He wanted to talk about us, which I figured. But we had a nice conversation, actually, and I think we're finally on the same page. John or no John, Sean and I just aren't meant for each other."

She nods her head. "Well, I know you had already moved on, but I'm glad at least he can move on now too, and you have some closure to that relationship." I nod in agreement, displaying the fake smile I've gotten good at showing.

When I first got back from Hawaii, I was wondering how our friend dynamic would change now that Sean and I were no longer together. When a couple breaks up, the mutual friends typically have to choose a side. Well, I guess while I was in Hawaii, they just naturally gravitated towards Sean. Most of them, anyway. There are a couple friends who are still making an effort to be friends with me, too, and of course, I still have Paige, but my friend group is drastically smaller than before I left. Even though it hurt my feelings at first, I'm all right with it now. I would rather keep my circle small and filled only with people I have a genuine friendship with.

"How's Hinge going for you? Any dates lined up?" I ask. Paige has been on a few dates through the dating app, and she always has entertaining stories about them.

"Ugh, no. I'm sick of dating. I give up," she says with a look of disgust. "Why is it so hard to date once you're out of college? It's like all the good ones are already taken. Hey, want to go see a movie tonight?"

"Oh, I can't. I'm having dinner at my parents' house tonight. Do you want to come? You know you're always invited."

"Sure! That sounds nice. I'll come pick you up from work." Paige is close with my parents, and she knows she doesn't need a formal invite.

We finish our salads, say a quick goodbye, and then I rush back to work to finish out the work day. The building I work in has almost entirely head to toe windows, and I have a nice view of the falling snow from my office. As usual, it's hard to focus, and I find myself wondering what John would have thought of the snow if he ever came here to visit. I think about how close I was to making a decision that would have so drastically altered my life. I was so close to saying yes to moving there. I was without a doubt in love with him. I'm *still* in love with him. That doesn't just go away.

I feel a twinge of guilt for leaving him when he clearly needs help. But at the same time, Paige was right—how much can I help him if he doesn't want to get help for himself? There's only so much I could do. I know I made the best choice I could for me, and I need to keep putting one foot in front of the other to try to move forward with my life, even though my heart still hurts.

I finish editing an article and send a few emails. The hours pass slowly, but eventually my phone dings with a text from Paige saying she's outside the building to pick me up. I shut my computer down for the day and close the door to my office. I say goodbye to a few coworkers that I pass as I walk out the doors to Paige. This is the best way I know how to put one foot in front of the other, and I keep clinging to the hope that the heartbreak will get easier over time.

26

JOHN

I've been staring at my phone for the last hour, trying to muster up enough courage to call. When Mia first left four weeks ago, I was absolutely devastated. I spent a full week in my bed. I was consumed with grief and let myself drown in it. I felt it all, slipping into a deep depression. I didn't really care anymore. I didn't have Mia to get out of bed for.

After that first week, I eventually peeled myself out of bed, forcing myself to shower and eat something. Since then, I've been slowly making my way back outside into the world. Cleaning the pool was at the top of my list. The following days I went to check on Rose, did some yard work, and even went to the beach a couple times. I didn't have enough energy to swim or surf, so I just sat there on the sand, looking out at the horizon, missing Mia.

I had to muster up enough courage to go clean the cottage. That was difficult, to say the least. Every inch of space in that cottage holds a memory of Mia that only served as a reminder that I lost her. She was gone. I miss her so much it's overwhelming, a constant ache in my chest that just got piled on top of the usual pain I live with every day.

A family from Texas came to stay at the cottage—a young couple with a small child. I could hear their laughter and chatter as they walked back and forth to the beach every single day. They were on cloud nine, enjoying their vacation in paradise as a family. It was such a stark contrast to the darkness I was living in right next door. I stayed inside my house the entire time they were here, successfully avoiding any in-person contact. They only reminded me that Mia wasn't here anymore. Once they left a few days ago, I kept myself busy by deep cleaning the cottage and doing some repairs. The family had mentioned on their check-out sheet that the shower head was leaking in the bathroom, so I fixed that, and I washed all the linens and towels to prepare for the next set of guests coming next week.

Since then I've had a lot of time to sit in my thoughts. I know that my brain is fucked up, and it has been for a long time. I know that I'm not even close to being happy. The closest I've come to normal was with Mia, but even though she made things less heavy for me, there was still an underlying darkness that followed me around.

I know that my brain has no idea how to process the trauma of what happened on that mountainside in Iraq. I know that I am not thriving on my own, and that I need to work through my issues or they will literally consume me for the rest of my life. I'm determined to become a better, more whole version of myself. Enough is enough. Losing Mia has forced me to be honest with myself, and confront the issues I was trying to bury. I don't want to feel like I'm drowning, or in an uphill battle the rest of my life. I'm not sure exactly how to do that, or what that will entail, but one thing I do know is that it starts with having a conversation with Adam.

So here I sit, still staring at my phone.

Okay. You can do this.

I blow out a deep breath, and scroll to find Adam's name in my phone. Just as I work up the nerve to hit the call button, my phone buzzes with an incoming call. Quinn's name lights up the screen. I let out a sigh. I guess if I'm trying to make an effort to let people in, not ignoring their phone calls would be a good place to start.

"Hi, Quinn."

"Hey!" She says in surprise. "I wasn't sure if you were gonna answer, it's been like a month since I heard from you."

"I know, I'm sorry."

A moment passes in silence, and then she asks quietly, "Are you okay, John?"

This is your chance, John. Let someone in.

I let out a deep breath. "Honestly, Quinn, no… I'm not okay. But I'm gonna work on it. I want to get better."

"What can I do to help?"

My stomach clenches with guilt. I don't want her to worry about me. But then I remind myself that I need to stop viewing myself as a burden. It's okay to let her worry about me, it means she cares. I have a feeling I'm gonna need as much support as I can get while I attempt to get through this.

"I'm not sure, but I'll keep you posted."

"Is Mia there with you?"

The mention of her name sends a fresh wave of pain through my chest. "No…she left a month ago."

"Oh," she says in surprise.

"I'll be all right, though… you don't have to worry about me, okay?"

"John, it's my job as your sister to worry about you. You're all I have left. It's you and me against the world, remember?"

Her words make me feel like a real asshole for always

shutting her out. Maybe she needs me more than she lets on. Who knows? Maybe we need each other.

"I know, and I'm right here. I actually have an important call to make, so I'm gonna go, but I promise I'll keep in touch, okay?"

"Okay... and John? I love you. Please let me know how I can help."

"I will. I love you, too, Quinn."

I hang up and suck a deep breath into my lungs. That felt good. Not that a whole lot came out of my talk with Quinn, but it was honest, and I didn't avoid her, which is a good start. Now that I have one honest conversation under my belt, I shift my focus back to the next one I need to have. I scroll back to Adam's number and hit the call button, trying to calm my nerves while the phone rings.

I hear a click, followed by a hesitant, "John?" His voice threatens to bring me right back to Iraq, but I do my best to push it out of my head.

"Hey, man," I say quietly, words suddenly stuck in my throat. I didn't plan out what I was going to say; I only knew that I needed to talk to him.

"How you been?" Adam asks, wariness obvious in his voice.

"Been better, I guess. You?"

"Same."

We let the silence fill the air for a few seconds, neither of us knowing what to say. Adam breaks the silence first.

"I've been trying to get in touch with you for months, man. Listen, I know you probably hate me. I just... I just need you to know that I didn't mean it, John. It was a mistake, I didn't mean to fuck up on the coordinates. I just—"

"I know."

"It was the biggest mistake I've ever made, the worst thing I'll ever do in my entire life. I feel so guilty, it fucking eats me

up inside. I took their lives and ruined their families' lives..."
His voice breaks.

"Adam..." I sigh. "I know. I mean, it was absolutely horrific, there's no sugar-coating it... but I know you didn't do it on purpose... and I don't hate you."

"You don't?" There's a sliver of hope in his voice.

"No. I mean, I'm obviously not handling everything well myself. I've got my own issues to work through, but I know that no good is gonna come from hating you." It's quiet for a few seconds, and I start to wonder if he's still there, when he finally speaks.

"Well... thank you... it helps a little knowing you don't hate me," he says quietly. I nod, even though he can't see me.

"Have you talked to any of the other guys?" I ask.

"A couple... I've tried to get in touch with everybody in our platoon, but I guess not everybody's ready to talk to me yet. Which I totally get. I spent the first few months after getting home in a really dark place, man. I couldn't stop drinking, trying to forget everything... I was a fucking mess. Langston got me in touch with a therapist, though. She's been helping a lot. She specializes in helping veterans returning home, especially ones with PTSD."

"That's great." I'm happy that he's figuring out a way to get help. "I really hope you work through your shit, man. You deserve to be happy."

"You do, too, man. Listen, I hate to do this, but I gotta run... I really appreciate you calling me, John, I really do." I can almost feel the gratitude coming from his voice, the sense of relief.

"Maybe I'll call again soon... good luck with everything."

"I'd really like that. You too."

I hang up the phone, spending a few minutes staring at my phone. It was easier to talk to him than I thought it would be. Once I pushed through the initial wall of nerves, it really wasn't so bad. I'm proud of myself for making that step that seemed damn near impossible just a short time ago. This is a good start. I open the sliding door and go sit by the pool. I let my legs hang in the water and feel the sun on my back. I start making a mental list of all the things I can do that might help pull myself out of this hole I'm in. I need to get a handle on my emotions, and then hopefully, I'll be able to function like a somewhat normal human being. I think of everything here in Hawaii that makes me even slightly happy and resolve to do more of those things if I can.

I'd also need to check in with Matt and Brian and let them know I'm going through a rough time, which is absolutely terrifying. Guys don't like to admit they need help, especially emotional support, but I'm desperate. I think of a few more things, but the very first and most important thing on that list is texting Adam to send me the name of his therapist.

27

MIA

Two months later

"Paige, I'm seriously dying to hear about the rest of your date, but I gotta let you go… I'm late for work; I'm just running out the door now." I scramble to slip my shoes on and grab the keys off the counter, holding the phone to my ear with my shoulder. I open my apartment door, back outside into the hallway, and lock my door, barely managing not to drop anything. I turn to rush down the hallway. "I'll call you after —" I'm unable to form any more words because when I look up, my eyes land on the face of the man I still miss so much that it physically hurts.

John.

He's standing at the end of the hallway, having just rounded the corner. My mouth drops open, and a shiver runs down my arms. I can feel tears already welling in my eyes. I don't know what he's doing here, or what he's about to say to me, but I'm so overwhelmed at just the sight of him.

"Mia? Are you okay?" Paige asks in my ear.

"Um," is all I can manage.

"Is it John?" she asks quietly.

She knew about this?

"Uh-huh."

"Okay, I'm gonna go... hear him out, Mia. Don'tbemadatmecallmelaterbye!" She hangs up in a hurry, and I don't have time to process her apparent deceit. John's eyes are still glued to mine, but neither of us has moved an inch. I take my phone and slide it into my pocket, my mouth still partially open in shock.

"What are you doing here?" I whisper. He seems to come unstuck, and he starts slowly moving in my direction. I wipe the tears from my face with my sweater sleeve.

"Mia..."

Oh damn, my heart. I missed that voice.

"Can I come in? I'd like to talk to you, if you have time."

I stand frozen in place, trying to form thoughts in my head.

"Um, well, I'm late for work..."

But screw work.

"I'll shoot my boss an email. Come in." I manage to pull my eyes away from him and turn around to unlock my door. Pushing it open, I go back inside the apartment and hold the door open for him. He walks in behind me, pushing his lips together and looking at the floor as he passes me.

Man, he smells good. He smells like warmth, salt, and everything else I desperately miss.

John takes the black bag that's slung over his shoulder and sets it gently on the floor next to the couch, turning to face me. I shut the door and pull my phone out to email my boss. I send her a quick message and look back up, not sure what I'm supposed to do next. What is he doing here? In my apartment? What the hell's going on?

"How are you?" he asks me. There's a softness to his voice that makes my knees feel weak.

"I'm all right. What are you doing here, John?" I cautiously move closer to where he's standing, stopping a few feet in front of him. I can't pinpoint it, but he definitely seems different. Lighter, somehow?

"I needed to talk to you."

"How did you know where I live? Paige, I'm assuming?"

He looks guilty. "Yeah... sorry, I didn't mean to be sneaky about it. But I wanted to talk to you in person. I found Paige on Facebook and she helped me out."

Good 'ole Facebook.

"She also told me you aren't seeing anyone else, or I wouldn't have come." His eyes shift down to the floor.

"Okay..."

"Mia... there's so much I want to say to you." He takes a deep breath, and his eyes lock with mine, looking directly into my soul. "I'm sorry it took me so long to come to you. I wish I could have come after you the second you walked out of my house; believe me, I wanted to. But I knew I wasn't good enough for you, Mia. I knew without a doubt that you deserved someone who could give you more than I could then, as much as it tore me up inside to admit it."

"Then why are you here?" My voice cracks, and I hate it.

"I've been doing a lot of work on myself over the past few months. I needed to make sure I was good enough for you before I came to see you. That I could be what you deserve. I've been seeing a therapist who specializes in helping veterans with PTSD."

What?

"You have?" I ask in disbelief, my brows lifting. My eyes fill with more tears. I'm just so happy that he's getting the help he needs.

"Yes. She's been helping me a lot. I've still got a long ways

to go, Mia, but I couldn't wait any longer before seeing you."
The tears start falling again, and my throat gets tighter. I look
down and wipe the tears, trying to make sense of my emotions.

"I love you, Mia."

My eyes fly back up to his. *He loves me?* I'm so shocked at
his presence and what he's saying to me that I can't seem to form
any words.

It's not lost on me how ironic this is. In an amusing turn of
events, John is the one pouring his heart out, and I'm the one
unable to speak. Go figure.

"I love you, Mia," he repeats. I can see his eyes starting to
get glossy and turn red. "And I don't just love you because you
make me feel less shitty. I love you because of who you are, and
that has nothing to do with my shit. I love *you.* I love the way
you make friends with everyone you meet, including Hazel, who,
by the way, told me to tell you that it's bad manners to leave
without saying goodbye. I love the way you love your family and
friends. I love that you love old classic movies, and that you're a
hopeless romantic. I love that you're optimistic and live your life
to the fullest. I love your bravery. I could go on and on, Mia.
And yes, I love the way you make me feel, but not because you
make me feel less miserable, but because you make every part of
me feel more alive."

A shiver runs down my spine.

He loves me. He's never opened up to me like this. Ever.

He starts to inch his way closer to me, and my heart starts
beating faster. His mouth slowly starts to turn up into a smile.

"Are you gonna say anything?" he teases me gently. All of a
sudden, my brain reconnects with my body, and I can't hold it
inside for a second longer.

I close the distance between us and throw my arms around
his neck, while simultaneously jumping and wrapping my legs
around him. I don't waste my time with words; I just press my
lips to his, and his grip tightens around my waist. He opens his

mouth and kisses me back, one hand under my butt and the other hand running up my back to rest on the back of my head. I feel like I can't get close enough to him, so I squeeze him as hard as I possibly can, trying to make up for the time we missed out on. Eventually, I break away and press my forehead to his, bringing both of my hands to his cheeks.

I look him in the eye. "I love you too, Jonathon Byrd. Now take me to my bedroom." His eyes sparkle, and his mouth curves into the biggest smile I've ever seen on his face as he carries me down the hall to my room.

"Is this real? Are you really here in Minnesota right now?" I run my fingers along his cheek and down his neck. We're lying in a mess of sheets on my bed an hour later, still clinging to each other, too afraid to let go. I gaze at him, scanning every inch of his face, taking him in. He looks so different. His eyes are less haunted now, but there's still a certain depth to them, like he knows what it feels like to carry the weight of the world on his shoulders. I could cry in gratitude that he's not suffering like he was.

"It's real. I'm here," he whispers.

"Did you really fly all the way here just for me?" I ask, and then another thought dawns on me. "What is it with people flying all the way across the country to surprise me, anyway?"

He chuckles. "Obviously, you're worth flying across the country for. You're worth it all, Mia. I mean, I didn't just get help for you… I knew I needed it, and I couldn't live like that anymore. But I was sure as hell praying that you'd be willing to take me back once I did."

"I couldn't stay away from you if I tried… the past few months have been complete torture. I missed you so much."

"I missed you, too." He grabs my hand and kisses the back of it. "And I'm okay with whatever you want to do with us. If you want to do a long distance thing until we figure out a more permanent solution, I'm good with that. Whatever you want to do. You're it for me, Mia. I'm not letting you go again."

I smile at him, surprisingly not feeling anxious about where we'll go from here. "We'll figure it out." We spend several minutes lost in each other's eyes, silently taking everything in.

"So... will you tell me who Adam is now?"

He doesn't even flinch at the mention of his name. He just nods, and tucks a piece of my hair behind my ear.

"I will. I'll tell you anything you want to know. I can't promise that it'll be easy for me to talk about, but I can promise that I'll try. I'm working on that. I want to be able to communicate with you, Mia. I want to be good enough for you. I want to *deserve* you."

I smile at him, and I take a deep breath. I don't press about Adam, because now I know we have plenty of time for all of that. It just feels so good to be back in his arms. I know with certainty that he is where I belong. He's my person, my home.

"Are you hungry?" I ask him. "I'll make you some food."

He nods. "Sure," he says. "I'll help you." We climb out of bed, throw our clothes on, and head to the kitchen. John helps me make some scrambled eggs and bacon, handing me utensils, flipping the bacon, and placing the carton of eggs back in the fridge. I'm reminded that we make a good team in the kitchen, although I can't help but wish I had some papaya to go with our meal. We stand, leaning against the kitchen counter across from each other and eat in silence, just staring at each other. You would think that seeing him in my apartment would make me imagine a life with him here, but it's actually giving me the clarity that I need. I'm suddenly confident in what our next steps should be. I set my plate down and cross the room to wrap my arms around his waist and look up at him.

"Ask me again."

His brows furrow together in confusion. "Ask you what?"

"Ask me to move in with you." His smile grows wider in understanding. He sets his plate down, puts his arms around my back, and brings his mouth to my ear.

"Will you move in with me, Mia?" he whispers, sending a shiver down my spine. I squeeze him tighter, look up into his eyes and smile.

"You betcha."

He grins and presses his lips to mine.

EPILOGUE

MIA

6 months later

"Heads up!"

I lift my head just in time to duck as a football whizzes past me, narrowly missing the folding table that I just set a bowl of fruit on.

"Jonathon Byrd! That almost hit the food!" I scold him. He runs over to me, kicking up sand behind him. He plants a firm kiss on my lips and places a hand on my hip, giving it a squeeze. "Sorry, baby. Won't happen again." He winks at me, retrieves the football, and runs back to throw it to Matt.

"Where do you want the chips?" Paige asks. I take the bowl from her and find a place for it on the table. This is Paige's second time visiting us since I officially moved to Hawaii five months ago. Each visit keeps getting longer, and I'm doing my best to convince her to move here, too. She says it won't happen, but that won't stop me from trying.

After John surprised me in Minnesota, things happened pretty fast. I gave my notice at work the very next day, and just a few weeks later, we had my apartment cleared out, and John and I came back to Hawaii together. My parents flew out with us to help get us settled, and they plan to come visit again in a few months. Of course, my mom was sad about me moving away, but she's supportive of John and me, and my happiness is what she cares about most.

I look out at the ocean and still can't believe I get to call this home. My heart swells with happiness. The beach, the sand, the food… I absolutely love it all. But not as much as I love the man I moved here for. I love John so much it freaking hurts. In addition to all the love, I'm also so dang proud of him and all the work he's been doing on himself.

He does a video conference therapy session once a week with his therapist, Dr. Kandry, who lives in California. She's been absolutely incredible. I've done a few sessions with him too, which was great. She helped give me some ideas on how I could best support him. He's come a long way. His friendship has deepened with a few of his close friends—Matt, Brian, Adam, and a couple other guys he was in the service with. He's also gotten closer to Quinn—we both have, actually. Quinn is like a sister to me too, now, and I'm happy to call her one of my best friends. We have plans to go visit her in Alaska next month, and she's actually planning to come here this year for Christmas, as well as their aunt and uncle. I feel so grateful for the support system that has truly rallied around John and been there for him.

He's even gotten back into doing things he used to love. The boys take him fishing every couple weeks—I graciously opt-out and let him have some guy time—and he surfs almost every day. He's even started teaching surfing lessons to tourists. I always sit on the sand a little ways away and watch him teach; it's one of my favorite things to do.

And, of course, we still manage the cottage for our Airbnb guests. John has to keep me from being too chatty with the guests, reminding me that they want their own space. I can't help getting excited and wanting to chat with everyone who comes to stay.

In between bookings, we even sneak over to the cottage every once in a while to cook and sleep for old times' sake. That cottage holds a special place in our hearts, and always will.

I spent the first several months here just getting settled into life with John, but now I'm trying to figure out how I can incorporate my editing experience here on the island. I have a couple leads for jobs in the field, which I'm excited about. I spend a lot of my free time at the bookshop, and of course Julie's. Hazel was thrilled to see me when I came back, and the feeling was definitely mutual. We have a standing Friday morning date at the coffee shop where we fill each other in on our weeks and plans for the weekend. Julie and Hazel come over every once in a while to swim in the pool. I'm not sure who enjoys it more, Hazel or John. That little girl has John wrapped around her little finger, and she knows it.

John's kiss on my cheek brings me out of my daydream. "What are you thinking about?" he asks me.

I smile at him. "Just how lucky I am."

He gives me a kiss on the lips this time. "I'm the lucky one." My heart skips a beat as I pull him in for a hug.

"Hey, thanks again for putting this picnic together," he says, wrapping his arms around me. "Matt and Brian kind of invited themselves along at the last minute... I think Matt might have a thing for Paige." He chuckles.

I glance over to where Paige is lounging on a towel, attempting to read a book. Matt is tossing the football up in the air to himself just a few feet away from her. He sits down and turns his head to her.

"Paige, you're looking a little lonely, sweetheart."

"In your dreams, Casanova," Paige replies as she sits up, brushing the sand off her legs. She walks over to us.

"Geez, does he flirt with anyone with two legs? He's more exhausting than my second graders..." she asks in amusement. I laugh and throw my arm over her shoulder. "Ahh, I'm so glad you're here, Paige."

She smiles at me, resting her head on my shoulder. "Me too."

"Girls, are you hungry?" John calls, placing a burger on his plate. We walk over to the table and make ourselves a plate of food. I bring my plate over to my towel in between Paige and John, and I enjoy the food while also enjoying my favorite view in the entire world—the ocean.

"Hurry, hurry!" I tell Paige as soon as we finish eating. "We have about ten minutes... let's hurry and clean up." We rush to put the food back in containers and into the cooler while John and Matt run our garbage to the trash can.

I quickly hurry back over to where John is sitting on his towel and squeeze myself between his legs, leaning against his chest, and he wraps his arms around me. I slide down a little bit, just until my head rests right under John's neck, securing me into my favorite spot: wrapped up in John's arms, watching the sun set over the water. Matt and Brian are throwing the football behind us, and Paige is next to us, reading her book.

I sigh, taking in the gorgeous sun appearing to sink into the sea as the turquoise water crashes softly onto the sand in front of us. I'm suddenly so grateful that Sean and I broke up, and that I came here all those months ago looking for clarity on the next chapter of my life. It all led me to this very moment, watching the sunset with John, and I'm so deliriously happy that I get to do it for the rest of my life. That, and an endless supply of papaya, are all I need.

The End

If you enjoyed Mia and John's story, please consider leaving a
review on Amazon and Goodreads.

ACKNOWLEDGMENTS

First, a very sincere thank you to you, reader. Thank you for taking a chance on my book, I truly hope you enjoyed it!

Thank you to Nick for your encouragement and support. Thank you for being my sounding board when I needed to talk through scenes or ideas, and for offering your input when I asked.

Thank you to Mom, Katie, and Erin for being my beta readers. Thank you for your encouragement, honest feedback and for never telling me to leave you alone when I asked you a million questions! :)

Thank you to my dad for sharing a love of reading with me, and to all of my family and friends for your excitement and support as well—it means the world to me!

ABOUT THE AUTHOR

Megan Reinking is a wife and mother who lives in Minnesota, where she spends her days reading, writing, or chauffeuring her three children around town. She's a homebody who loves quiet, lazy days and connecting with family and friends. The Ohana Cottage is her debut novel.

CPSIA information can be obtained
at www.ICGtesting.com
Printed in the USA
BVHW040328250522
637943BV00005B/511